GLIMPSE

JANE HIGGINS

TEXT PUBLISHING MELBOURNE AUSTRALIA

The Text Publishing Company acknowledges the Traditional Owners of the country on which we work, the Wurundjeri People of the Kulin Nation, and pays respect to their Elders past and present.

textpublishing.com.au

The Text Publishing Company
Wurundjeri Country, Level 6, Royal Bank Chambers, 287 Collins Street, Melbourne Vic 3000 Australia

First published by The Text Publishing Company, 2023

Cover design by Imogen Stubbs
Cover design incorporates imagery by PSDGraphics/Creative Market
Page design by Rachel Aitken
Typeset by J&M Typesetting

Printed and bound in Australia by Griffin Press, an accredited ISO/NZS 14001:2004 Environmental Management System printer.

ISBN: 9781922330598 (paperback)
ISBN: 9781922459114 (ebook)

A catalogue record for this book is available from the National Library of Australia.

The paper this book is printed on is certified against the Forest Stewardship Council® Standards. Griffin Press holds chain of custody certification SCS-COC-001185. FSC® promotes environmentally responsible, socially beneficial and economically viable management of the world's forests.

For Ruby-Jane and Kit

PERCHED ON ITS eggshell crust of earth, the city shook like a drunk in need of a drink.

The earthquake turned the ground to shifting silt and filled the air with the dust of fallen buildings. After-shocks followed. No day went by without a jolt. And not just in one city, but in all the cities that lay on the long track of the ruptured fault.

People ran for a time on adrenaline and goodwill. They mourned their dead. They looked after their neighbours. They prepared to rebuild. But the after-shocks kept coming—thousands of them, years of them. Whole districts were declared too dangerous even for demolition, presenting people with a bitter choice: leave home forever, or hunker down and hope for an end to the shaking and the beginning, one day, of the rebuild.

After seven years of aftershocks it was easy to despair.

But there was this too, like a gift from the rubble: across the city a small number of people began to see the earthquakes coming. And that made warnings possible. And endurance. And hope.

There were others, though, who watched the despair and the hope and they saw easy prey and a pathway to money and power.

1

JONAH WAS THE quiet one, and watchful too. He had his reasons. Bas, though, he liked a brawl—jump now, think later, that was Bas. He had the kind of staying power that didn't hurt till afterwards, once he'd left his opponent sprawled in the dust. And Evie was a firebrand, clever and fierce. But she wasn't there on the night it all kicked off.

It began the way work nights usually began. Jonah met Bas on the church steps in Linden Plaza at the heart of the Demolition Zone. Until the quakes began seven years ago, the neighbourhoods and streets of shops around the plaza had been the city's Downtown East, but now that whole area was scheduled for demolition, hence, the D-Zone.

On the top step you could look across the plaza and down the long—and long-destroyed—main street where buildings broken open by the first big quakes had spilled their guts in a cascade of dust and rubble and work-a-day stuff: a mangled mess of desk tops and chair legs and paper, lockers leaking running shoes and lunch boxes, laundered piles of waitstaff aprons, framed photos of kids and dogs, bicycle wheels with handlebars bent right through them, certificates of Employee of the Week and Manager on Duty still attached to their broken walls.

It had all been picked over long ago, of course, first by looters then by the rats that swept in like an all-conquering army and fed themselves fat on the cafe spoils that lay rotting in the winter sun. With them came the clouds of blue-arsed flies. The buzz of those flies: it got inside your head so that even when you couldn't actually hear it, your brain got to work telling you that you could.

Then came the spring rains, and the summer winds that blew the rubble dust into everyone's lungs, until more rain settled the dust, and as the seasons rolled on, the place was almost washed clean.

These days only worthless trash was caught up in the rubble of the buildings around the plaza—beer cans, plastic bags, ripped-up sofas, three-legged tables and two-legged chairs—all dumped there while people went looking for a better class of trash on the next block over and the one after that.

Over the years since the quakes began, Bas and Jonah had sat for hours on those steps. They played cards on long, boring afternoons, they dissected the tangle of which gang boss was on top this week, and they planned where they'd go when they'd saved enough money to get shot of this place.

The day's rain had moved west over the city, but the clouds were still heavy above the D-Zone and the last of the sun was lighting their underbellies purple.

'Jeez,' said Bas, trotting up the steps to the top where Jonah was waiting. 'Did you get that one just now? That was a little punk.'

Jonah grinned. 'Wake you up?'

It had been a solid jolt. And Jonah had seen it coming, glimpsed it, the way he saw all of them coming—the ones bigger than about a magnitude three, anyway.

Bas pretended outrage. 'Piss off!'

'Where were you?'

'At home. On the roof.'

'The roof. Naturally.'

'I was looking at that leak. Near as dammit fell off. How big was it? Four? Four point five?'

'About that.'

'I mean I could wait till a glimpser was nearby before I did any damn thing, but the place would grind to a frigging halt if we all did that.'

The plaza was busy, the night market setting up. There was the usual jangle of gaudy confusion thick with chat and laughter. Strands of tiny lights were being strung from stall to stall. Molly Peyton, smoothing her length of faded green felt across her table, laid out silver and bronze jewellery and brand-name watches that were as genuine as the 'licensed' software that Stringer Jones was selling next to her. Here you could find stalls that would sell you T-shirts signed by saints and celebrities, rugs handwoven by grandmothers and virgins, tattoos to protect you from surveillance satellites, sheet music written by angels channelling dead men's songs; you could have your fortune told, your enemies cursed, your unborn children blessed and your dead assured of paradise.

Jonah and Bas walked into the market batting greetings back and forth and seizing on freebie morsels of food. The market fitted them well, like the faultline tattoos on their faces and the battered, rubble-ready boots on their feet.

They were cousins: their mothers were friends who married brothers. In the days before Jonah could remember, Bas's dad lit out to a different town and a different family, but their mothers stayed close and Jonah and Bas grew up like brothers themselves. They were thin, like a lot of people in the Zone who didn't have a full stomach often enough, their brown-black hair was cut short now and then, and both of them had that tattoo, the branching line snaking from temple to cheek, shaped like one of the faults in the web of faults that had broken nearly seven years ago and crashed their city to the ground. The tattoo had become the mark of the D-Zone—the sign you wore to show that this was your patch.

The market stalls where Jonah and Bas worked were up already, their owners busy and grumbling, not unkindly, about 'the youth', and why couldn't they turn up on time and how was it possible to run a business when you were beholden to sloth of such magnitude. Pizza My H'Art, where Jonah worked, was basically a pizza oven on wheels, but Art's pizzas were legendary. Tonight, he'd set up beside Carlotta's Luck Candles—*Get a Handle on your Luck!* On Art's other side, Nemy was well into his work stuffing potatoes and grouching at Bas for turning up when most of the night's work was over already. Bas snorted. It was barely half six and it was bitterly cold—it had all the makings of a slow night.

Opposite Pizza My H'Art was a Glimpse Corporation stall. It had only been at the market a month or so and Jonah had chatted a couple of times with its attendant. She was in her early twenties, her name was Shikha Doran and she came with a bodyguard. Every evening she travelled across from the GlimpseCorp tower in the central city, set up her stall, stayed a couple of hours, and then went back through territory that Jonah wouldn't hang around in longer than absolutely necessary, even in the daylight. Hence, the bodyguard.

The stall was there to advertise the Glimpse Show, a flashy reality-TV program where people who had glimpses relived their experiences and underwent intense personal questioning by the show's resident psychologist to work out why they had glimpses. This was followed by the high point of every show: emotional encounters with people whose lives they'd saved through their timely quake warnings. There were rewards, mainly gifts of the sponsors' products and, for those participants who were really popular, there were the inevitable sponsorship deals and social media celebrity.

Shikha was at the night market to enlist participants. No surprise, she wasn't having any success. Jonah wondered if he should put her out of her misery by explaining that a lot of people in the D-Zone didn't have citizenship papers and were regarded by the authorities as illegal immigrants. Which meant that a tell-all show exposing who they were and where they lived was never going to be a winner.

By half ten, Shikha was long gone and Jonah was on his bike, a tower of pizzas strapped behind him, heading for Needle's fortress of Ruskin Flats. Needle was one of a feuding set of local gang leaders. Jonah knew most of them; he'd even gone to school with a few. These days his only contact with them was pizza delivery. They never tipped. They were tougher than he was by an order of magnitude; also, they could and would deploy weapons when riled. Jonah didn't have weapons; his version of self-defence was a fast getaway. These guys dealt in stolen goods and drugs, and also construction crews, which were hard to come by in the D-Zone.

By eleven Jonah was sitting on the steps of Ruskin Flats feeling his ribs after Needle's security boys had asked where the freebie was: hadn't they ordered the half dozen? And wasn't there always a freebie when you did that? Jonah made the mistake of explaining that that was last week's special, but Needle's boys took against this idea and indicated their disappointment by kicking him down the steps. Unpaid. Because, for a man to pay for his pizzas after being insulted like that in his own fortress, well, wouldn't that show a shaming weakness of character?

Across the street, a couple of glimpse obsessives huddled in a doorway, out of it on whatever Needle was peddling today. Obsessives were usually out-of-towners desperate to turn themselves into glimpsers. They were easy prey for local gang bosses. These two had watched Jonah's kicking like it was a stunt for their entertainment. Jonah waved at them and called, 'Thanks!' but they stared back, dim-witted and empty-eyed.

When he could stand up, Jonah got to his feet, grabbed his bike and headed back to Art.

He was almost back at the night market when a

sound he hadn't heard in years sailed across the sky.

A saxophone. Music he knew in his bones.

It soared above the shrill and clatter of the market, trilling, diving deep and climbing again, over and over, high, wild and sorrowing. It swept the night sky like a searchlight. Jonah stopped beside Irondog's Demolition Bonanza: *Nails, Knives and Knuckles! No Questions Asked!* No one was at the Demolition Bonanza except old Irondog himself. In fact, no one was at any of the market stalls except their owners, who were grouching because their would-be customers had been distracted from buying stuff. A marquee had gone up across the front of the church steps and about thirty people were milling in front of it.

The marquee was black—such a deep midnight black that you had to look twice to see it there; it had none of the stripes and flags and stuck-on stars that fancied up the rest of the night-market stalls. At its entrance, a single glowing globe hovered in the air, held up by nothing that Jonah could see. It drifted now and then with the movement of people passing by.

The saxophone's song was so lonesome it made you stop and think of the ones who were gone. Over the last seven years, loss had become as familiar as hunger, but bringing the lost to mind was a gift too, because it put you right back with them, before they were taken by the quakes, and it gave you permission for the tears on your cheeks and the loneliness that grabbed at your gut.

Irondog noticed him. 'Close your mouth, kid. It's nothing good.' He spat on the ground. 'It's PANN.'

Jonah nodded. His voice had dried up.

Irondog swore. 'People for a New frigging Nation.'

'I know who they are,' murmured Jonah.

'Some New Nation. Pan-dae-mon-i-um, more like.' Irondog pronounced it like it was five words. 'We don't need their sort here, you know that, right?' He spat again. 'I'm packing up. I don't want trouble.'

Jonah didn't want them here either. But the wail of the saxophone across the stalls was like a wind on his face, blowing in from faraway places. He could tell the crowd felt it too; there was a buzz, as though people knew something was coming. He moved off around the edge of the market, keeping to the shadows, watching.

It had been years since PANN had first shown up in the D-Zone and last time it happened, well, it hadn't looked like this. The last time was Quake Year 2, when Jonah and Bas were twelve. Jonah remembered running—he and Bas, both—to catch up to the crowd that was gathering to see what was going on.

Back then, PANN had arrived with a trio of brightly painted house buses and a few dozen people wearing blue and white tunics bleached pale from long hours on the road. They walked alongside the buses ringing small bells. Jonah remembered the strangeness of that sound.

In a neighbourhood whose daily soundtrack clamoured with hammers, buzz-saws, pneumatic drills and the occasional gunshot, that gentle chime of bells seemed to promise another world.

But that was a long time ago. Jonah wondered if things were different now. When he reached the black marquee he hung back, wondering if they'd show up: the pale woman, Phaedra, and her blind brother, Damon.

'Gimme your hand, boy.' Madame Clara, the clairvoyant, had come out of her tent beside the marquee and grabbed Jonah's hand. She shone a little torch into his palm, muttering at what she saw. Eventually she closed his fingers over his palm, patted his hand and peered up into his face. 'Don't go in there, lad. It'll only give you grief.'

Too late, he thought. Far, far too late.

Madame Clara nodded as though she understood then wrapped her shawl around her and retreated into her tent.

A tall, pale woman dressed in a long blue tunic stepped out of the black marquee. It was her. Phaedra. Jonah edged back into the shadows. Five years ago, his twelve-year-old self had watched her climb down from a brightly coloured bus in Wulfstan Wood and captivate her audience. Back then she was the most striking woman he'd ever seen. And nothing had changed. He couldn't see her eyes in the dark now, but he remembered them well: they were electric blue. Her skin was paler than pale and her eyebrows and lashes were white, like her hair. His twelve-year-old self had been entranced. His seventeen-year-old self, not so much. He wondered where her brother was.

Back then, in their beauty and mystery, the sister and brother had cast a spell across the broken land of the D-Zone and the broken spirit of its people. And, Jonah realised, they were still doing that. They shone in a way that made everything around them look grey and dull in comparison: the night market lights strung between stalls looked like what they were—hot wires inside plastic baubles, the flags were tattered and the buntings torn and dirty, the signs for Pizza My H'Art and Nemy's Hot Potatoes were rough stencilled whitewash on bent and splintered plasterboard. The air stank of food that had been charred or over-boiled. It was sad and dreary and even he couldn't love it right now.

Phaedra looked out across the crowd, smiling and inviting people inside. Jonah wanted to march out of the shadows and implore them not to go in, but his feet wouldn't move and he could only watch and listen.

Phaedra's voice was as musical and warmly inviting as ever. 'Come in! Come in! Relax. Lay down your troubles. You'll find rest here, and a promise of so much that is to come.'

Watching the queue move, Jonah recognised tiny

Paulina with the orphan Mina who was always at her side. When they reached the head of the queue, Phaedra cupped a hand under Mina's chin and smiled into the little girl's eyes then put an arm gently around Paulina's shoulders and ushered them both inside. And then came Louisa, whose brilliant sewing fingers brought old clothes back to life. Phaedra held both hands out to her as though she were a long-lost friend. Then she summoned a young man from inside the tent to assist old José, hobbling over his walking stick. And when she saw Jean Pierre with his arm protectively around his fragile and very pregnant partner, Mae, she gave a small cry of delight and ushered them in.

And all these people had a light in their eyes as they looked at Phaedra. It was more than curiosity, Jonah thought. It looked disturbingly like hope.

'Ladies! Gentlemen! Friends from the past, and friends newly welcome!' Phaedra was lifting her voice now, inviting the whole market to hear. 'Welcome to our New Nation! Are you anxious about the earthquakes? Come on in. Are you worried about Border Control? Come in. Money troubles? Wounded in love? Family problems? Come in. Come in. We understand your worries. Come and lay them down here. Because right here, with People for a New Nation, you will find a truth that will set you free.'

She stepped aside to allow more people to enter the

marquee. Then she saw Jonah. She gestured towards the entrance. 'Come in. There are wonders inside.' Her voice was gentle. When he didn't answer, she walked towards him and it took a surprising amount of willpower for him to stand his ground. Her eyes narrowed, puzzled. 'Have we met?' she asked.

His voice stuck in his chest.

She smiled. 'I'm sure we have. I never forget a face.'

But she had, he thought. She had forgotten.

There was movement at the marquee opening; her brother appeared and Jonah's throat tightened. Damon hadn't changed either: as tall as his sister, as thin, as pale, but with eyes white and clouded. Phaedra turned back towards him and took the hand he offered, like a queen to her king. She murmured, 'Someone we've met before.'

Damon turned towards Jonah. 'Invite him in,' he said.

'I have, sweet. He won't come.'

Jonah clenched his fists in his pockets.

'Ah!' Phaedra lifted her head, eyes glitter-bright. 'I remember now. The glimpse boy. Yes.' She dwelt on the word. 'What a dear child you were. And with such a gift. Do you have it still?' As she spoke her smile slipped and Jonah could have sworn that for a moment, her blue eyes went dark and her mouth turned hungry. She moved towards him extending a graceful hand. 'Come. You carry so much pain. I see it. Let me help. Come inside.

Be free of what troubles you.'

Jonah almost choked on the words surging in his throat but he couldn't find his voice or the right words. He wished Bas was here. Or Evie. They'd know what to say. They'd know how to shame these two with the truth. How to send them packing.

Phaedra, gestured again towards the tent. 'These are your friends, your neighbours. Don't be left out in the cold. Because this?' She glanced at the queue, then back to Jonah, 'This is just the beginning. Wait till you see.' When Jonah didn't move, a tiny frown appeared in her colourless brows. 'No? Think carefully, glimpse boy. Make sure you are on the right side when the time comes.' Then she took Damon's arm and walked back inside the marquee.

Jonah realised he was shaking.

2

JONAH MADE HIS way back to Art's. The old man looked up from loading a pizza into the oven, bushy eyebrows raised, bushy moustache twitching. 'What gives? You okay?'

No, thought Jonah. 'I guess,' he said. 'PANN's back.'

'Hard to miss. They do love to put on a show.'

Jonah pulled on an apron.

Art studied him, frowning, then looked back towards the black marquee. 'What do they want with us again, I wonder.'

'Nothing good,' said Jonah, opening a container of grated cheese. 'Where's Bas?'

Art frowned as he scattered mushrooms on the next pizza. 'Hey, Nem! Where's that boy of yours?'

Nemy waved tongs in the air. 'On a break.' He looked at his watch. 'A half hour he's been gone! I don't pay him to take a half hour of a break. You see him, you send him here, pronto!'

Art ripped a page of completed orders off his notepad, scrunched it up and held the pad out to Jonah. 'Are they hungry in that marquee? Let's get in there, eh?' He pointed in the direction of the crowd then raised his eyebrows at Jonah. 'For some reason, you're still here.'

Jonah took off the apron, grabbed a pen and jogged across to the people milling around the marquee. He was in the middle of taking an order when he saw Bas coming out of the entrance. Jonah stopped.

His customer said, 'Hey! My order!'

Jonah said, 'Sorry. Can you…I'll be back in a minute. Sorry.'

Bas was standing still, looking far ahead, as if he was seeing right out to the cracked smokestacks on the city boundary.

'What the hell?' Jonah grabbed his arm.

Bas turned a blank stare towards him then rubbed a hand over his face, blinking. 'Jo. Hey.'

'What gives? Why'd you go in there?'

'Huh?'

'What are you doing?'

'Doing?'

'Going in there!'

Bas shrugged. 'Nothing. It's nothing. Looking. You know.'

Jonah's eyes narrowed. The marquee entrance was still devouring people. Bas held up both hands. 'Hey. Be cool, okay? I just went to look. Nothing wrong with looking.'

The sax wailed, full-throated and gorgeous.

Jonah glared at the marquee so he wouldn't glare at Bas. His friend was fragile these days. 'You know what they are,' he said.

'Course I do. But they haven't been here since…I dunno, years. Maybe they've changed—you never know. I just went to look.'

Jonah walked away but Bas caught him up and slung an arm round his shoulders. 'Wait. Wait up…Don't go all angsty on me.'

Jonah pulled away. 'Did they give you something? What'd they give you?'

Bas opened both arms wide. 'They gave me nothing, okay? Not a thing. Wouldn't take it if they did.'

'Bas.' Jonah was pleading now. 'You think they give a shit about you? You think they care about anything except their own sweet selves? They don't even—' He swallowed. 'You better get back to work. Nem's fierce you disappeared for so long.'

'Jeez. Lighten up.'

But Jonah was walking back, staring at his pizza orders.

'It was a bit of fun,' Bas called. 'What's wrong with a bit of fun?'

Nothing, thought Jonah. Everything.

Six months ago, Bas had lost his mother, Rebecca, and little sister, Lily, to a quake. They were crushed under a falling building that should have been fenced off—but this was the D-Zone and no one official was monitoring what was safe and what wasn't any more because everyone was supposed to have left by now. In the months since, Jonah had seen Bas drunk and raging, drunk and weeping, drugged to the eyeballs and insensible, also hyper with fury and paralysed with sadness. But having fun—no, he hadn't seen him having fun. How could he resent that?

But this was PANN. They were back and Jonah knew they hadn't changed. He turned around. 'It's not fun,' he called, 'when it's PANN!'

Nemy was furious when they arrived. 'Do I pay you to stand around and gossip? No. I pay you to prep potatoes. Do I see you prepping potatoes? I do not.'

'Easy, old guy,' said Bas and he laughed at his own bravado.

Jonah turned away and everyone got back to their work and there was no more talk except what was necessary, and no more backchat either.

Jonah ran pizzas until 2.30 am when Art pressed his night's pay into his hand and sent him off. 'Go! Sleep! We're done here. What are you waiting for—you think there won't be more tomorrow? Believe me, there'll be more. And, Jonah!' Art waggled a finger towards the midnight marquee. 'Don't let those people get to you.'

'Sure,' Jonah nodded, but as he turned away the marquee filled his view. There was no queue outside it now and the saxophone's lonely wail had fallen silent. Jonah sipped a can of cola and watched the entrance while he waited for Bas to finish work. The globe still glowed, but it was the only sign that someone might be inside.

At last Bas was finished. Jonah eyed the cash as Bas pocketed his wages. 'Nem dock you?'

Bas grinned and shook his head. 'Must've forgot.'

Jonah thought kind thoughts towards the old guy for not making a big deal of Bas disappearing in the middle of his shift and then giving cheek on top of that. He shouldered his backpack and turned to pick up his bike.

Bas said, 'I'll catch you up. Just got something to do.'

A knot twisted in Jonah's gut. 'It's closed,' he said, looking at the marquee.

'Yeah, it's not that. Something else. See you at home.'

Do you call out your best friend because he's just lied to you, or do you let it slide and hope that you won't remember in the morning? Jonah scrunched the can he'd just finished and threw it hard towards the marquee.

'They can go back to hell where they came from,' he yelled. But Bas was already walking away. Jonah's heart lodged somewhere in his boots. He picked up his bike and thought about heading for home. But his brain was too busy for sleep.

He jumped on his bike and sped away from the plaza. The streets he was racing down were broken and unlit, but he knew every corner, every crack and pothole, every pile of rubble—and every gang fortress. All of that was easy to dodge. He charged through the night, the air ice in his lungs, until he reached the old brickworks on the edge of the D-Zone where he and Bas used to hang out when they wanted to get away. There he stopped, heart thumping, exhilarated by the dark and the cold and this temporary escape from the things that weren't easy to dodge: PANN was back and someone had to call them out for the frauds that they were. Jonah didn't want to be the one that did that. But Bas, it seemed, wasn't going to be either. Bas showing an interest in PANN gave Jonah a shitload of worry.

3

AT DAWN, JONAH turned for home. The cloud cover was still low and heavy, but the sun was rising beneath it, shooting brilliance down the alleys of the D-Zone and lighting up slabs that were once walls connected to other walls and were now eerie reminders of buildings that used to be. The early morning, when the sun shone glory on the desolation, was Jonah's favourite time of day. He shared it with his dad—he liked to think that, anyway. He figured he was coming home at the same time his dad was heading out to work in some other city.

His dad left a few years back to go and work in the rubble in quake-struck cities in the north where the money was good. He travelled from city to city, job to job, but he sent money regularly. And birthday cards and new year's greetings, always with wishes for good things in the year to come.

For that reason, Jonah liked to be alone this time of day. He wasn't troubled that the souls of the earthquake dead might be walking along beside him. This was home to them, that's what his dad taught him, just like it was home to the living. They could share the streets, he didn't have a problem with that.

He wheeled his bike down Old School Road, walking behind his shadow to the end where he climbed a fence and dropped down into a garden, lifting his bike after him.

The garden was neat in a busy sort of way with rows of spinach and chard, and pumpkins swelling on their vines. Beehives lined the back fence and there were chickens too, but they were still asleep, cosy in their boxes in a big wood and wire-netting coop that Bas and Jonah had built. There were apple trees, lemon trees and bushes that grew thick with tiny jewel-like currants, black and red, in the summer. It was a small green space that thrived amid the desolation of the D-Zone.

'Jonah. Hey.' Evie looked up from spreading compost between the rows and leaned on her garden fork. She didn't say, 'Where have you been?' or try a line like 'You must have worked real late?' She didn't even look at him slant. She just stood in the middle of the vegetables and smiled at him.

She was older than he was by a year or so, and she sang a gorgeous alto in the church choir. This rambling old building with its runaway garden was her home, and his too since her family had taken him and his mother in after the quakes began.

In the first years of the quakes, Evie had taught Jonah how to play the guitar. Sitting with her on the church steps, he'd fallen fast for her bright eyes and broad smile, her hair, glossy as a chestnut, caught back from her face in two clasps, her cheek smooth in the sunlight as she leaned over her guitar, strumming like she was born to that music.

Every summer when the linden trees in the plaza filled the air with their sweetness and the heat rose from the pavement under his bare feet, Jonah was reminded of those times: the way Evie bent her head to explain the chords, her long lashes lowered in concentration as she played them through for him, one by one, until he had them.

He loved to hear her sing. Some people sing as if they know the answer and here they are giving it to you. Others sing as if they're searching—there is a question in their eyes, on their face: can you help me understand this song? That was Evie. Always, she was having that conversation with the people listening, even if it was only him.

'Hey.' He kissed her. 'Bas come home okay?'

She raised an eyebrow. 'Funny thing. That's just what he asked about you an hour or so back.'

'Oh.'

'Something going on between you and Bas?'

He hesitated. 'Kinda.'

'You want to say?'

'You hear that sax last night?'

'Sure did. Pretty, wasn't it.'

'It's PANN. They're back.'

Evie stabbed her fork in the ground and gave him her full attention. 'Well, well, are they now.' She pulled off her beanie and ran a hand through her hair. 'Bas didn't tell me that.'

'I saw them, Phaedra and her brother. Bas did too. Bas went…anyway, why are they back? We don't want them! They're fake and everyone knows it!'

Evie studied him for a moment then pulled her beanie back on. 'Does everyone? I'm not so sure, and I bet they say different. Full of big promises all coming to nothing, were they? Did you talk to them? Tell them to get lost?'

'Sure.' He bent his head and kissed her neck. 'Gave them this big speech, telling them people won't be so gullible this time. No one's going to fall for their bullshit. You know. Like I always do. I take my job protecting the Zone from fraudsters seriously.'

She grinned and turned to put her arms round his neck. 'Yeah, that's you all over. Telling people where to get off. Yelling at them, even. The number of times I've heard you yelling at people to quit their bullshit. No, wait, that's wrong. I've never, ever heard you yell at anyone.'

'You should've been there. You would've told them.'

She shook her head. 'Maybe. You could too, you know. Yell, once in a while.'

He rested his cheek on the top of her head and closed his eyes.

'Seriously, though,' she pulled away and looked up at him. 'People won't pay much attention. We got our own battles to fight. BCB's on the move. Three families yesterday. Just bashed their doors down and trucked them out to Flint Point, no explanations, not even any paperwork as far as we can tell. It looks like the start of a new campaign.'

Before the quakes, the Border Control Bureau had come often to this area, known then as Downtown East. No one knew how many people in Downtown East were without citizenship papers, 'illegals' as the BCB called them. Plenty, was the general understanding. And there was no doubt that the Bureau planned to find every one of them and move them out.

Jonah and Bas, for instance, were born right here, and they could prove it but that wasn't enough. Their parents had come from over the sea and they'd built lives for themselves without being a bother to anyone. No matter that Jonah's dad was willingly breaking his back in the rebuild of another city; no matter that Bas's mother had spent the early quake years helping people who had no one else to call on. They had no papers. Therefore, they weren't citizens. Therefore, they were fair game for the BCB to cart them away to the camp at Flint Point where they could rot for years before being sent back to where they'd come from, even if they could hardly remember where that was, even if they had never actually been there.

Since the quakes, the BCB had left the D-Zone to itself. There'd been other punishments for illegals: no vouchers from City Hall for quake counselling and education, no repair or relocation funds, or any other kind of help. But at least there'd been no raids. Maybe the powers-that-be thought it was all too dangerous, and why bother anyway—why not leave the place to be slowly destroyed by the quakes and its own gang warfare?

'So,' Evie was saying, 'We got no time for PANN right now. They'll come and go and no one will even notice they've been here. You'll see.'

'I dunno,' said Jonah. 'They've got fancy—glow globes and music and shit. People like that kind of stuff.'

Evie frowned and Jonah said what offended him most. 'And they sound…they sound really fine.'

Evie's smile was wry. 'The devil gets all the best tunes, that's what they say. You should go to bed. I've got practice.' Choir practice, she meant.

Since the first quakes, the choir had become much

more than a bunch of people singing in a church. It had become a voice that everyone in the neighbourhood turned to for solace and fortitude. No matter its crazy practice schedule that didn't give a hoot for anyone sleeping within three blocks of the church. No matter the gospel leaning that not everyone took kindly to. The music was the only thing of beauty in the empty-headed chaos of the quakes.

The choir's songs would spill down the church steps like a joyful, mournful, shining river, flowing into the plaza where people stopped still and listened: songs about surviving your troubles and taking care of your neighbour, about struggle and hope, about grieving your loss. And as the quakes kept coming, the songs called for holding on and standing strong together. The choir lifted people up and carried them through the queueing and the water-carrying, the makeshift toilets and the pitch-black nights, the prep drills and the memorial services.

People began to realise that it was not only builders and plumbers and sparkies they needed, but music-makers too.

Then the Suits came, and everyone said, *At last, the Suits! Now we'll get some action!* And the choir sang about hope and rebuilding your life on a firm foundation. But when the Suits announced that Downtown East was not going to be rebuilt and City Hall said there'd be no help for those without citizenship, the music turned defiant.

In the years since then, the choir had held regular fund-raising concerts and waged information campaigns to rally people to fight for, and with, those who were deemed 'illegals'.

'You've got practice now?' said Jonah. 'Since when was dawn practice a thing?'

'I know, right?' said Evie. 'Since my dad decided we ALL had to be there. It's hard to find a time that suits everyone. And you know what he's like: the original stickler.' She pulled Jonah close and kissed him, her brown eyes warm and full of promise. 'Go sleep. I gotta get going. I'll catch you later.'

Jonah and Bas were ten when the first quake ripped through the city. It was a Saturday afternoon and they were in their space-rocket tree hut in the backyard that their terraced houses shared. That afternoon they were on a mission to the Moon and everything was looking good but then the engines roared for real beneath them, twisting and bucking them from their seats and pitching them both, yelling, out of the tree. They landed, still yelling, on the lurching ground, followed by the planks of the tree hut, and they watched the line of houses where they lived crack from roof to basement in clouds of dust and tumbling brick. There was a moment when the crashing stopped, but then car alarms and building alarms and sirens ripped across the city and the ground shook again. The boys dug their fingers into the grass and clung on as though that grip was all that stopped them from sliding off the face of the earth.

Jonah didn't remember much more of that day, except that his mother had a crack on the head and his dad got called to help in the rescue effort downtown. Bas's mother, Rebecca, sat with the boys and Jonah's mother and they waited for the medics to come. Jonah, watching his dad go, felt proud and did not cry. Rebecca cried though, just a little, then she sat holding his mother's hand where she lay semi-conscious on the backyard grass with a coat spread over her. But although they watched all afternoon and into the evening, the medics did not come.

The earth shook and groaned all that night. No one slept, except Jonah's mother, and no one managed to calm the screaming babies or the crying kids from neighbouring yards. Sometimes, after a big aftershock, people would shout at the darkness, as though the earth might hear them and calm the hell down, but it just kept on rolling and roaring. Jonah badly wanted his mother to wake up and his father to come home but he tried not to let on that he was worried.

It was a huge relief when, a week later, Rebecca asked Evie's mother for help, and Jonah and Bas, along with their parents and Bas's sister Lily, came to live in the old schoolhouse that Evie's family was converting into a home.

It was a rambling two-storey place made of timber, so every time there was a quake it shook like a weed in the wind, but it didn't fall. Evie's family called it the Matterhorn because, she told Jonah, the quakes put such a slope on the floors that you needed crampons like a mountaineer to get from one end of it to the other. He and Bas helped in the work to turn some of the rooms into more bedrooms for other quake refugees, and they dug up the schoolyard to expand the vegetable garden and orchard.

A lot of things went right for them, for a while. In Jonah's memory those days were a strange weave of the terror and weirdness of his first glimpses and the comfort of that house: his dad coming home each night, his mother safe asleep upstairs, the crackling warmth of the log fire in the living room, the aroma of soup steaming on the kitchen stove, people turning up at all hours, sometimes for soup, sometimes just for company. And there was Evie, of course.

A few months went by, then the Suits turned up again and told everyone that the whole eastern stretch of the city was a demolition zone now and everyone had to get out. But not everyone had somewhere to go, and there were those, too, who dug their toes into the silty shit that the earth had vomited up onto their streets and they made it plain that they were staying put.

Bas's mother, Rebecca, spent hours at the Quake Recovery authorities pleading for money to set up a school for the quake kids who lived near the Matterhorn. But she always returned empty-handed. Once, in a rare fit of temper, she told Bas and Jonah, 'And what did they say this time? They said, No! Of course they did. Because that's what Suits are paid to say. It's in their contract, or in their blood, one or the other, and if they even once say, "Yes, that's great, what a fine idea, of course we'll help you," then they vanish in a puff of sulphur and inciner-ated dollar bills.' Then she'd stopped and looked at their wide-eyed expressions and she'd smiled. 'Don't worry. We'll work something out. We always do, don't we?'

And they had. The Matterhorn team had managed well, glad to offer food, shelter, friendship and basic schooling to the shattered people of the D-Zone.

Then six months ago, a quake took Rebecca and Lily away forever.

4

IT WAS MIDDAY when a glimpse woke Jonah. Waking or sleeping, his glimpses were a nightmare of falling from an impossibly high ledge into a roaring darkness. Splinters of light came at him as though he'd been pitched into an exploding mirror. That tumbling fall stole his breath and made him retch, but what kept him from utterly dreading his glimpses was that each piece of broken light held a bright, sharp image. It had taken him months to work out what he was seeing but he knew now that it was fragments of landscape—the same landscape in each glimpse, but different depending on the time of day and the season.

There was a shingle riverbank, a cascade of water flowing over stones, trees with long bending branches dipping into the river. Always he felt the air on his skin; sometimes it was cold and fresh, sometimes hot and dry.

Often, he heard a burst of birdsong above the roar.

He had no idea what this landscape was. Everyone had a theory, and Jonah's was that this was the land as it used to be millennia before they built the city, and it was coming back now to remind him, to remind them all, that the earth belonged to itself and not to the people who thought they owned it.

A kick of fear hitched a ride on every glimpse, and then Jonah was back in the world, gasping, and waiting for the quake to arrive. You could never tell exactly how long it would be, but it was usually minutes. There was often enough of a gap that he could stagger upright and shout a warning for whoever might be nearby.

Today's quake came on too fast for that. Jonah curled into a ball and hoped it wasn't going to get so big that he'd have to move to the doorway in case the ceiling collapsed. He felt too sick to move. When the shaking withered and died he blew out a long-held breath. Once the panic had passed, he did the breathing exercise that Evie's mother had taught him to calm his nausea, then crawled out of bed. He felt like he'd been hit by a truck. Bas's bed was empty.

There was no one in the kitchen which suited Jonah fine. It was lunchtime but he made porridge anyway, ladling it into a bowl with a drizzle of honey and milk, then he took it up to his mother.

When Jonah came downstairs he found Bas in the kitchen sawing at a loaf of bread.

'Hey, Jo. Glimpse get you this morning? You okay?'

'Yeah. Nah, I'm fine.'

Bas frowned at him. 'You look like shit.'

'Cheers.'

The thing about Bas was, you had a fight and next day it never happened. Bas didn't stew on things. Jonah was not so good at leaving arguments behind. 'What was in the marquee?' he asked.

Bas raised his eyebrows then shrugged and layered pickles on his cheese sandwich. 'Stuff. Like last time only fancier. Glow globes, lots of those. Big ones and little ones, all just floating there—really cool. And there was pilgrims—that's what they're calling the followers.'

'Pilgrims. That's weird. Why are they called that?'

'Dunno. Something about making a journey here, I guess. They think the D-Zone is special somehow. And what's-her-name was there. Fay...?'

'Phaedra.'

'Her. And the brother. She looked just the same as last time.'

'Yeah. It's creepy. Did you talk to them?'

Bas sat down at the table and took a bite of his sandwich. 'She talked to me, a bit. Said she remembered me. I dunno—how could she? Anyhow, everyone's all blue clothes, white hair now. Like they're all trying to be clones of those two. There was a heap of people going through.'

Jonah started making his own sandwich. Someone had made bread, which used to be Aunt Rebecca's thing. She'd taken on the kitchen to help Evie's parents when they had so much else to do helping quake refugees and she'd made it the welcoming heart of the household. After she died it had become a place that you hit when you were hungry. But it was still welcoming with a big log burner and a long table with benches either side. On weekends Jonah ate lunch there with Evie and her family. Now, he sat down across from Bas, who said, 'How's your mum?'

Jonah shook his head. 'Okay. Same. Why are they here, do you think?'

'Well,' Bas dragged out the word and hesitated. 'They're signing people up. I mean, I didn't, but…'

'Signing them up for what?'

'I dunno exactly. To become pilgrims, I think? There's different levels—you know, there's entry level and I think a couple of other levels before you get to batshit crazy—that's the real hard core, the blue clothes, white-hair types.' He crossed his eyes and stuck out his tongue which made Jonah smile.

'I bet you have to pay?' said Jonah.

'Pay?' Bas grinned. 'Are you kidding? A donation, they called it. But you don't get to join without it.

Anyway, they were talking about some project they're planning and if you sign up you get to be part of it. But they wouldn't say what it was. Gonna be a big reveal, I guess.'

Jonah shook his head. 'Or not. Seriously, why'd they come back here? What do you think?'

Bas finished his sandwich and got up to put the cheese and pickles in the fridge. 'I dunno. Look, they might all be gone by tonight. Especially if no one signs up to their special brand of weird.'

'Good riddance,' muttered Jonah.

'Yeah. I guess.'

That evening, Jonah and Bas were late for work and they ran the last few blocks to the plaza, but when they arrived nobody gave them half a glance. Everyone was there but no one was doing a damn thing. The stalls weren't up, the skin artists weren't at work, the fortune tellers and purveyors of oddball blessings weren't touting their fringe brand of luck, and the sellers of T-shirts and caps and shoes and every other trash thing that got sold in the market hadn't unpacked their merch. Everyone was crowding the edge of the plaza.

'Holy shit,' said Bas. 'What the hell?'

Jonah spotted Art and they elbowed their way through to him; there were tears on his face and he wasn't wiping them away.

'What the hell?' said Baz again, louder.

No one had gone into the plaza because the plaza was already crowded with people standing shoulder to shoulder. Not real people. Transparent. Translucent. Astonishing. Statues of light.

'Holograms,' breathed Jonah. He looked at Bas. 'Are they?'

Suddenly Art walked into the crowd of statues, and his movement was like a spell broken; people swarmed after him, Bas and Jonah too.

As they walked, peering into the faces of the holograms, Bas said, 'It's one heck of a publicity stunt, but who did it and what for? It's freaking amazing—hey, hey, hey, wait a sec.' He stopped in front of two small shining statues standing close to each other. 'Jo? Back up? Who do these ones look like?'

'Jeez.' Jonah came to stand beside him. 'Maggie and Jack.' The twins from the fruit and vegetable shop on the corner of Blunt and Randal; they'd all grown up together, before the quakes. They'd ridden their bikes out to the smokestacks on the edge of town, played ball in the carpark out back of the disused brickworks, gone to movies and ballgames together. Jonah and Bas stood and stared. It was Maggie and Jack, no doubt about it. Caught in a laughing moment.

Jonah put out a hand and touched the light of Maggie's face as if he expected her to look up at him, smile and reach out. He pulled his hand away.

'How, though?' said Bas, his voice edgy. 'What's going on?'

'And there's Sam,' said Jonah, pointing. Sam who had run the bakery on Alton Street. 'And Alicia.' From the vet clinic on Holden.

Bas looked around them, 'Are they all…They're not. Are they?' He ran down to silent.

'Yeah,' said Jonah. 'They're all dead. The quake dead.'

'Holy—I mean, what?'

People walked around them, searching in every shining face, crying out when they found someone they knew, weeping, laughing with joy and disbelief.

'It's a miracle! A miracle!' said someone behind them.

Jonah turned to Bas. 'D'you want to get outta here? Because I sure do.'

'Yeah. In a minute?' Bas was wandering among the holograms, studying the faces.

A woman weeping hard barrelled into Jonah knocking him sideways and when he recovered his balance he'd lost sight of Bas. He yelled his name, but it was too noisy and too crowded so he made for the church steps, thinking that Bas might head there too. He couldn't hurry; he had to be careful to not walk through one of these memories-made-real. You could, if you'd wanted, put your hand right through them. You could drop to the ground and crawl about, searching for the transmitting devices that made them possible. And you could curse it as a terrible trick played on innocent quake victims, alive and dead.

But no one did any of those things.

The quake dead stood still, gazing into forever, while their living families and friends stepped among them, dazzled and bewildered.

Jonah arrived at the church steps where Art's beloved Lucia stood, as though she had every intention of climbing the steps and going to a service. Art stood before her, weeping openly. Jonah had no words for him.

'Jonah!' Evie came racing over to him. 'Isn't it wild? Come on—we'll get a better view from up top.' She pulled on his arm, hauling him to the top of the steps where they looked out across the crowd. The holograms were brightening as the dusk deepened. Waves of people were flooding in.

'Hell of a thing,' said Jonah.

'Kinda is,' said Evie.

'It's gotta be PANN. Bas said they were planning to launch some big thing. I guess this is it.'

'Now of all times.' Evie blew out a breath. 'We got the BCB banging people's doors down and what do we get from this lot? Cheap tricks and woo nonsense.'

Jonah was silent. Cries of delight and the sounds of weeping floated up to them. Then Evie pushed a hand through her hair. 'Okay, woo nonsense was harsh.'

'Probably wasn't cheap either.'

'But you know what I mean. It's so frustrating. Right now, we need to be fighting the BCB. We need to be looking for evidence to prove that these raids are unlawful. We've got Corner Store Law helping us out. I mean, they're not hopeful, but at least they're working on it. We need people to be focused on that, not spaced out on…on *this*.' She raised her arms at the crowd in exasperation.

'You can't blame them,' said Jonah, watching to see who he knew down in the crowd. 'Whoever's done this wants to get under our skin. Let's hope it's gone by tomorrow.'

'Please let it be gone by tomorrow!' said Evie.

'Bas is down there.'

'I know. Do you think his mum…'

'Sure of it.' Jonah knew with a cold certainty that holos of Rebecca and Lily were down there and that Bas would find them. Bas's grief was a huge, complicated, unfathomable work in progress. Maybe finding them here would help, but maybe it would unravel all the work Bas had done so far. Jonah knew about grief work—everyone did. Knowing about it was one thing, but doing it—well, they called it work for a reason and people in the D-Zone had been hard at it for a long time now. Could years of grief work be undone in an hour?

A helicopter hovered above, searchlights weaving. Evie looked up at it. 'It's about perfect, isn't it? What a way to bring us to our knees at last. We can protest the raids, we can laugh in the face of the red tape, we can dig in and refuse to move until we get fair treatment…I used to think we could defend ourselves against anything. But what's our defence against this? It feels like it's opened its mouth and swallowed us whole.'

'You think it's Border Control?'

'Or City Hall? They've surely run out of patience with us still being here. I don't know. I mean how does some weird little cult like PANN get hold of tech like this?' She shook her head. 'Whoever it is, they expect to suck us in with their fancy lights, and while everyone's looking the other way they'll swoop in and clear us out.'

'Couldn't it just be a promo by PANN to sign up members?'

Evie looked at Jonah, eyes bright. 'Let's ask them.' She turned around and found Damon, the blind brother, standing right behind them.

'Whoa!' Evie squared her shoulders and lifted her chin. 'Do you mind not creeping up on people like that?'

He ignored her and tilted his head back as though he was surveying the crowd through those sightless eyes.

Evie said, 'Why are you here and when are you leaving? No, actually, I don't care why you're here. Just when you're leaving.'

'Leaving?' Phaedra came through the doors of the church, smiling, and stood beside her brother. 'Why would we leave? People love us.' She looked at Jonah. 'You loved us once.'

Evie glanced at Jonah, but he didn't speak.

Three young men, dressed in the same blue as Phaedra and Damon, came out of the church and stood behind the brother and sister.

Evie frowned. 'What are you doing in there? Why are they—'

As she spoke the signature sound of the saxophone swelled from inside the building.

'We're making music,' said Phaedra. She turned to the three young men and said, 'Thank you. That sounds perfect.'

'Wait a second!' Evie was fuming now. 'You don't get to take over this building.'

'We can. And we have.' Damon's voice was cold and flat as an iron blade.

But his sister spoke over him. 'It's a community space, open to everyone.'

'It's open to community-minded people,' said Evie. 'I don't think that includes you. Are you going to help us get citizenship for people who've lived here all their lives? Or stop the BCB raids? Or get hold of quake assistance for people who've lost their homes? Any or all of the above? Because if that's not what you're here for, then you're not welcome.'

'I think you'll find that we're very welcome,' said Phaedra. 'Imagine if we left and took this gift with us.' She gestured to the statues of light. 'Because that's what it is. A gift from us to the people of this place. Now why don't you run along and find your friend.'

'Run along!' said Evie. 'What, are we six years old? And what do you know about our friend?'

Phaedra looked at Jonah. 'More than you might think.'

A chill ran down Jonah's spine. 'C'mon.' He took Evie's hand. 'Let's go.'

'No, wait!' Evie turned to Phaedra. 'Who's behind this. Who's paying for it?'

Phaedra held Evie's gaze and said softly, 'Benefactors. People who wish you and your people well.'

Evie snorted. 'Benefactors.' She glared at Phaedra for five cold seconds, then turned and charged down the steps muttering furiously all the way. 'How dare they! Who do they think they are? Who do they think *we* are? There's gonna be trouble if they think they can set up in the church, let me tell you.'

Once they got into the crowd it was slow going; people kept stopping them, wanting them to marvel at the holo figures, wanting to tell the story of what their beloved mother or father, son or daughter, sister or brother, friend or lover was doing when their image was captured like this.

They found Bas at last, sitting on the ground in front of the holo of his mother and little sister who stood arm in arm, smiling, their eyes lifted as though they were about to greet someone. The likeness hit Jonah hard. It really was them. He crouched down and put a hand on Bas's shoulder, wanting to pull him away. But Bas was still and staring and no pleading was going to move him now. Jonah sat next to him. 'Bas?'

Bas turned shining eyes towards him, and Jonah knew it was too late.

5

IN THE DAYS that followed, the holograms drew growing crowds. Every evening as the sun set and the holos began to glow, people streamed out of their houses to see this miracle. It was like a parade, with people talking excitedly as they joined in, but then the talk got quieter and quieter and they arrived at the holograms in near silence.

Outsiders began turning up too, drawn by the holos and by PANN's cryptic promises of a new world, which they delivered nightly to packed rallies in the church.

Then one morning, about a fortnight after PANN arrived, Evie shook Jonah awake. 'Jonah! You have to come with me.'

Jonah peered blearily at his watch. 'It's 8 am.'

'Get dressed. Hurry.' She slammed his door on her way out and called 'Sorry!' from the hallway as he flinched and hauled himself groaning out of bed. '8 am!'

he called back. 'Did I mention?'

'What?' he said as they left the house. 'What is worth getting only four hours sleep for?'

'This is important.'

Arriving at the plaza, they climbed the steps to the church and she threw open the doors. 'Look!'

He frowned. 'Oh. I'm guessing you didn't do this?'

All the seats had been removed, creating a large open space. Giant speakers had been hoisted high and wired into the walls. The choir's crappy keyboard, that used to crouch in the corner like an oversize bug, was gone. The ropes that marked off the place where the choir sang and swayed and clapped, letting loose the wild beauty of its music, were gone too. And lines had been painted on the floor delineating an aisle and boundaries within which, Jonah guessed, people were supposed to stand during the rallies.

'Have you complained to them?' asked Jonah.

'Dad's off doing that now. He wouldn't let me go with him. Said something about diplomacy. But we just need to see them off, it's as simple as that.'

They went back outside. The holos were glimmering in the grey, wintry daylight. Evie crouched beside the holo of Art's wife, Lucia, and peered around its base.

'What are you doing?' asked Jonah.

'I want to know how they work.' She glanced up at him. 'Looks like they're on a small platform and probably if you lifted that up…'

'Evie!' said Jonah. People were gathering around them.

'Mm?' She was feeling around the edges of the platform.

Jonah tried again. 'Evie!'

'What?' She looked up impatiently. 'Oh.' She held up both hands and stood up, smiling brightly. 'Just looking.'

'Looking for what?' said a man.

'To see how they work. They're lovely, but they're not a miracle, you know. I mean…' She looked at Jonah who was standing at the back of the group. He stared hard at her and shook his head a fraction, but he knew this was hopeless. Evie was on a case. There was no point trying to dissuade her.

'Look,' she said to the people watching. 'I'm just worried that people are getting distracted from the real danger right on our doorstep. Border Control is on the move here and—'

'Let me tell you something, little girl.' The man stabbed a finger in her direction. 'We don't need your help. We got protection.'

'What d'you mean?' said Evie. 'You don't mean PANN? They might be very good at taking your money, but they're not going to save you. The BCB will still come knocking.'

'Well, that's where you're wrong,' said the man. 'We're

gonna declare ourselves a New Nation. BCB won't have any power here anymore, you'll see.'

He turned to the people around him, now a sizable crowd. 'Yeah? Am I right?' There were murmurs of agreement from some in the crowd, frowns from others.

Evie started to say, 'That is such bull—' but Jonah cut in saying, 'Thanks, we're just leaving.' Evie gave a disgusted shake of her head and marched off through the crowd.

When Jonah caught up with her, she said, 'Why did you do that?'

'Because something ugly is happening here. But we don't know enough about it yet.'

That evening as Jonah and Evie were making pumpkin soup for dinner, they heard Evie's dad come in. She raced out to see him. When she came back she said, 'They made him wait a whole day to see them. Bastards.'

'What's the gist?' asked Jonah.

'He asked politely and they told him to take a hike. Not in so many words, but…'

She counted out soup spoons. 'How many are in tonight? You, me, my mum and dad, my pesky brother, your mum, Auntie June and Uncle Raynor. That's eight. I don't think Bas is in?

'People are buying it though,' she went on. 'That's the worrying thing. Even Bas. He told me that we shouldn't be fighting the BCB. We should be working towards more important things. He might have even said *higher things,* for God's sake, but I think I excised that from my memory. And so I said to him, mightn't he feel differently if the BCB turned up on our doorstep and hauled the both of you away. And he said—the same as that guy today at the holos, actually. Someone's coaching them. Anyway, he said that people who signed on with PANN had nothing to worry about because PANN can protect them? God knows how. He's getting in thick with them. I'm worried about him.

'Plus,' she continued, 'People are complaining that we, as in the choir, are not joining in with their message of *hope*.' Her fingers made air quotes around the word. 'I mean, I'm all for hope.' She lifted soup bowls out of a cupboard and put them on the table. 'I hope the BCB falls over its own bootlaces. I hope City Hall finds an unexpected pot of money in some corner or other that's tagged for the D-Zone to help us get back on our feet. You know, boring things.

'What I don't hope for is a fantasy future that we all just step into one day where our beloved dead are back with us as though they never left.' She blew out a breath and went to put her arms around Jonah, resting her head between his shoulder blades. 'What do you hope for?'

He turned around and kissed her.

He felt her grin, then she said, 'No, but listen.' She

stood back. 'This is serious. People don't trust us anymore. I'm worried.'

He looked at her fierce expression and shining eyes and was afraid for her. But that wouldn't stop her taking on anyone and everyone if she thought it was necessary, so there was no point telling her that.

After they'd eaten, Jonah headed to work. The night market, upstaged by the holo-shrine, was a remnant of its former glorious, if downbeat, self. Stall holders set up in narrow spaces on the edge of the plaza. Art and Nemy were there, but Art's mind was not on pizza-making; these days he left that to Jonah so that he could spend time with the holo of Lucia.

Jonah's mind wasn't much on pizza-making either. He knew Evie was right to be worried about Bas, who had progressed from sitting in sad contentment at the feet of his mother's holo to hanging out with the pilgrims. There was only one night in two that Bas turned up to the Matterhorn to eat or sleep. And at Nem's stall he arrived late, left early and sometimes didn't show at all. He was full of excuses and promises, but excuses and promises didn't bake potatoes.

Jonah helped Nemy out when he could; Nem's wife died years before the quakes began and he was silent on the subject of PANN. Most people, however, were not silent. They were excited, fascinated and awed and they wouldn't shut up about it. Jonah, in a minority of not very many, was shaken by this.

He felt unmoored. Bas was wrong to be following PANN, and Jonah had the scars from last time to prove it, but the more he argued the deeper his friend dug in.

Tonight, Bas came over as things were getting busy and leaned on the counter of Pizza My H'Art. He grinned at Jonah like everything was fine. 'How's it going?'

Jonah was kneading dough. 'Okay, I guess.' The three small tables were occupied and there were people standing nearby scanning the chalkboard menu. 'Could use some help.'

Bas glanced at the customers. 'Yep, sure. Later, for sure.'

'Now would be better.'

'Uh, hey,' Bas looked back towards the holograms where the crowd was building and pilgrims were wandering about talking to people.

Jonah's gaze flicked up then went back to his dough. 'What?'

Bas leaned in and said quietly, 'Listen—'

'Nope.' Jonah knew this tone. 'Not PANN. Too busy. Don't care.'

'But—'

'I got work to do. If you're not gonna help…' Jonah started shaping the dough.

'I know, I know. And yeah—there's work to do, all

right. But not this.' Bas waved a hand at Jonah's pizza-in-the-making. 'This is…we got much more important work. Just *listen* for a sec, okay? I can explain. How many years is it since Quake One?'

'Bas, don't start.'

'How many?'

Jonah shook his head. 'Seven, give or take a few days. So?'

'And d'you know how many big roads lead into the D-Zone?'

'What?'

'Seven! And holos! How many holos are there in the plaza here?'

'Eighty. We counted, remember? Why am I playing this stupid game?'

'No! Not anymore. They took three down cos some people broke the rules and losing a family holo was their punishment. Now there's seventy-seven.'

'Of course there are.'

'It's all converging.' Bas's eyes were bright with excitement. 'The quakes. The glimpses—seven letters in glimpse, by the way. What's that all leading to? That's what we gotta figure out. *That's* our work.'

One of the customers was listening, frowning. 'You're scaring my customers, Bas,' said Jonah.

Bas leaned in, talking fast, stabbing a finger on the counter. 'Listen, you're the one who gets the glimpses, right? Do they make sense to you? No. And why do the quakes keep coming years after they started—does that make sense? No.'

'No, and who cares?' Jonah put a pizza on his long-handled paddle, sliding it into the oven. He grabbed his next order and started on it.

'I care,' said Bas. 'And PANN cares.'

'Jesus, Bas!' Jonah dropped his voice to a hiss. 'No, they don't! The BCB are on the move. And look where they're moving: last three weeks they've been in Midgeway Park, Broadview, and yesterday in Ledner's Row. What does that look like to you?'

'I dunno—'

'Yeah, you do. All those blocks are northeast of the plaza. They're concentrating their efforts. They've got a plan, I'm telling you.'

'Okay, okay.'

'Next, they'll be knocking on our door.'

'But listen. We got twenty-seven days till the anniversary—'

'Losing people to the BCB is important *cos it's real.* This other stuff? It's bull.'

But Bas was looking towards the plaza again as though he was hoping for reinforcements. Jonah turned to check on the pizza in the oven.

'Listen,' persisted Bas, 'The…the glimpses—they're our clues! We have to use them to work out what's going on, what's gonna happen. So, we have to share them, right? If we all share them, we can make a picture of what's coming. Twenty-seven days. Then a new world. Don't you want to give it a chance?'

So PANN was glimpse-hunting, Jonah realised. That was why Bas was standing here. Not because he wanted to see Jonah, or pick up his job with Nem. And what did PANN want with people's glimpses? What they'd always wanted, of course. Power. Control. They would build up their aura of mystery and importance if they were able to say, *Look! We're gathering this strange, life-saving gift of glimpsing to ourselves. We alone truly understand it.*

Jonah wasn't going to give them anything.

'C'mon!' said Bas, as though he was expecting Jonah to down tools on the spot. 'We need you! Come and help!'

'Or what?' said Jonah. 'Or their big surprise won't happen? Is that it?'

But Bas turned away, looking towards the plaza again. Jonah's heart sank. He'd heard the rumour, of course— who hadn't? On the seventh anniversary of Quake One—which was, as Bas said, in twenty-seven days—a last mighty quake was going to rip through the whole country, generating huge energy and the D-Zone would be ground zero. And then…and then…something or other, something vaguely extraordinary apparently. They talked up the creation of a New Nation—an independent D-Zone, as far as he could tell—but there were other, darker hints behind that talk that he knew Bas and a lot of others were hoping for.

Jonah leaned on the counter and gave Bas his full attention. His friend's wide-eyed hope was hard to bear. 'Don't do this,' he said. 'It won't happen. The holos are just holos, that's all they are, that's all they'll ever be. They're never gonna wake up. They're just tech, Bas. They're just a clever bit of tech.'

Bas stared at him hard, then looked away. 'Know that, do you?'

Jonah shook his head. 'Yeah, I do. And so do you. And so does PANN. They're a con, pure and simple.'

He turned to shovel the pizza out of the oven.

'They've changed,' said Bas. 'I'm telling you. You gotta let all that other stuff go. Past is past.'

Jonah scribbled down a new order and smiled his thanks to a customer while he delivered change. 'Did they tell you to say that?' Jonah asked. 'Your new friends? Past is stupid past? Go away. I'm busy.'

But he took time to glare at Bas walking away and didn't hear a new customer ordering pepperoni with extra pepperoni.

Later that night Evie joined him at one of his tiny gingham-clad tables. They ate a pizza and watched the holos shine. The plaza was almost deserted because everyone was in the church listening to Phaedra's weekly Words of Wisdom.

Evie leaned in close and lowered her voice. 'That girl over there on the GlimpseCorp stall? What's her name?'

'Shikha,' said Jonah.

'Her bodyguard's gone to look at the rally and she looks lonely and hungry. Let's invite her over.'

Jonah nodded. 'Sure, why not?'

Shikha was happy to join them. After they'd introduced themselves and had the obligatory conversation about how freaking cold it was, Evie said, 'You didn't want to join your security guy at the rally? It's warmer in there, at least.'

Shikha smiled. She had curly hair, dyed bright red and crammed messily under a woolly hat, her eyes were dark with smoky eyeshadow, and her smile was nervous. Once she'd finished a slice of pizza, she pulled up the collar of her coat and held it close with gloved hands. 'To be honest,' she said, 'he's not supposed to leave me alone, but I get tired of his grouching so I told him to go and check it out. I figured there's hardly anyone around, and I'm not selling anything so no one's gonna rob me of cash I don't have.'

Evie finished her pizza and wiped her fingers on a napkin. 'If you're not selling stuff, what are you doing?'

Shikha sighed. 'I'm trying to recruit for the Glimpse Show. But no one's interested. I thought people would be falling over themselves to be on it, especially here…' She trailed off.

'Especially here?' Evie prompted.

Shikha grimaced. 'Sorry. I just thought, what with all the quake-prone buildings and gangland feuds and Border Security raids? Why wouldn't people want out? Sorry, it's none of my business. I'm supposed to be finding glimpsers but I'm starting to think there aren't any here. Are there? Do you know?'

Jonah could feel Evie looking at him but he avoided her gaze and nodded towards the church. 'They're in there, mostly. If you believe the PANN schtick, glimpses are kind of sacred—some sort of window into a new world or the future or something.' He shrugged. 'Which means, I think, that going on a glimpse show to win, I don't know, a handful of cash…? Well, that would be selling out the glorious future that is certainly, definitely, maybe, happening any day now.'

Shikha studied him. 'People here love PANN. Why don't you?'

Jonah gave a choked-up laugh and Evie said to him, 'You should tell her. You want people to know what they are, don't you?'

6

'IN THE FIRST quake,' Jonah told Shikha, 'my mother got hit on the head when the chimney in our house fell through the roof. We waited all night for an ambulance to come.'

'No one came?' asked Shikha.

Jonah shook his head. 'She got put in a shelter but it was, you know, so busy, then she got shifted to a temporary hospital but the doctors there couldn't help her. They said give it time. Be patient.'

Shikha nodded. 'What happened?'

'PANN.' He started tearing a napkin into symmetrical pieces. 'PANN happened.'

'They've been here before? I didn't know.'

He gestured into the dark of the D-Zone beyond the plaza. 'All this…it'd all been condemned and everyone was supposed to be getting out. People were going crazy—do they stay, do they leave, *can* they leave? Anyhow, one day PANN arrives and marches down Boundary Road with their people clinking their little bells and they go right up to the gates of the wood—which were locked to stop people camping there, even though it was an obvious place to camp if you'd just lost your house—and they walked right in. I don't know how, I don't remember. They must've got the key from someone, but it looked like magic to us. What did we know? Anyhow, they go right in and set up this huge tent, I mean *huge*, like it's got a whole universe inside, and they invite us in, and they promise…man, what didn't they promise. They promised everything. They were gonna fix the world.'

'You must've been just a kid.'

'Twelve. Bas and me. We thought they were magic—what with the walking through locked gates, and the man being blind but seeming to see, and her being just as queen-like and strange as anything. And they *promised…* they promised to help. They said they had healing hands and all kinds of crap like that. And I believed them. I thought, right, I've got someone you can help. So I took my mother to them. We went to the magic people in the magic tent and we said to them, *Hey, here's someone you can help.* And they said, *yeah, we can help, but we need a donation. And the more money you got, the better the help we can give.*

'I went…I knew where my dad was saving all our money, to pay for her to go someplace to get proper treatment. He was pulling double shifts and working all hours. And putting the money in a box—because where do you put money when you can't have a bank account because you don't have papers? But it was taking so long to get her any treatment. Too long. So I took the money. About fifteen grand.'

He paused, shook his head, then went on. 'I took all the money and I went back to the tent where she was waiting. And they said thanks and took her away to do some kind of mumbo-jumbo over her. And a couple of hours later they brought her back and they said: *Look! She's better now.* And I said, *No, she's no different.* And they came back with some bullshit like, *She might not look it, but she's ascended to a higher fucking plane of existence where she's happy and it would be wrong to bring her back.*

Jonah stopped and a little silence fell.

Shikha stirred. 'That's evil. That's plain evil. You were twelve years old, for crissakes! What twelve-year-old wouldn't do exactly what you did?'

'A smart twelve-year-old,' said Jonah.

'Did you get the money back?'

'My dad tried. But PANN upped stumps and left and that was that.'

'Where's your dad now?'

Jonah folded his arms. 'We were broke, thanks to me, so he had to go and work in other cities, where there's money, so we could get medicine and therapy for my mum.'

Shikha sat back. 'Con artists, pure and simple.' She hesitated then said, 'I don't suppose you glimpse?'

Jonah looked at Evie. 'Why?'

'Because,' said Shikha, 'that's a hell of a story. If you came on the Glimpse Show, you could tell it to the world.'

Later that night, Jonah and Evie sat on the couch in the Matterhorn living room and Evie said, 'Why didn't you tell her?'

'Because I don't want to go on her stupid show. I bet they don't take illegals anyway.'

'And I bet they'd find a way if you had a good enough story to tell. Which you do.'

The next Sunday, Evie's pastor father preached on the church steps to small, loyal crowd about the dangers of believing false prophets, especially when they were offering fantastical answers to people's troubles and charging a fee for them. The Sunday after that, when the congregation was even smaller and the voices upholding PANN were louder than ever, her mother preached directly about PANN and their so-called New Nation that could never happen, no matter what the seventh anniversary brought in twelve days' time.

There was no night market on a Sunday so Jonah spent the evening with Evie, curled up on the couch. They talked quietly, not about the days that were gone; other people could hash over those times. They talked instead about the future, when the quakes would end, when all the houses in the D-Zone would be rebuilt, when Jonah's mum would be back to who she used to be. Evie wanted to talk about Bas too but Jonah wouldn't. 'If he wants to be an idiot, I can't stop him,' he said.

'Do you think he's signed on as a pilgrim?'

'Maybe. I don't care.'

She poked him gently in the ribs. 'You care.'

'He doesn't want to be here, that's pretty obvious. It's his life. He can do whatever—Shee-it!'

The bay window had shattered in an explosion of glass and a brick hurtled into the room and thumped down right by the couch.

Evie yelled, 'What the—!' and grabbed at the back of her head. Her hand came away bloody.

Her dad, who had been in the kitchen, dashed in, swore and took off outside. He was back soon, breathing hard and shaking his head. 'No one's there, of course. Are you kids all right? What was it? A brick? Let's see it.'

Evie's mum arrived with the first-aid kit saying, 'Careful! Let's get you out of all this glass.'

There was piece of paper wrapped around the brick.

'What does it say?' asked Evie as her mum dabbed at the cut on Evie's head.

Her dad frowned and held it out to her mum who took it and said, 'Oh!'

Evie and Jonah peered over her shoulder. It was a hand-drawn image of a house with a wide front veranda and high dormer windows—clearly the Matterhorn—engulfed in flames. Across the image were the words: TWELVE DAYS.

7

SHIKHA SAT BACK in her chair and looked interested. This had become her default face, which was useful for work, but outside of work it had the unintended effect of encouraging far too many people to tell her far more than she could possibly want to know about the minute detail of their lives.

Right now, though, in the closing stages of a workday afternoon, it was minute details she was after. Anything to make the day less of a write-off. The man sitting on the other side of her desk reminded her of a grandfather from central casting; bushy eyebrows, grey hair thick as a broom, and a broad, blunt face without a hint of sly.

'You say it looks green?' prompted Shikha.

'Well…' He nodded slowly. 'Kinda.'

'Kinda?' she mirrored his nod and offered a small smile.

'Sure. It looks kinda green. And … leafy? With, you know, sometimes there's sunlight or some-such?'

'Trees? Are you saying you see trees in sunlight?'

'Sure. Sunlight. Maybe?'

'You don't sound very sure, Mr McHugh.'

'It's over that quick.' The man snapped his fingers. 'That's why they call them glimpses, I guess. There's the green and the light and I don't know what-all else. Maybe something else is there too—something moving?'

'Animals? Try to think, Mr McHugh. Try to recall.'

'I been trying. That's all I got. Do I qualify?'

Shikha gave an inward sigh and wriggled her toes in her boots, reckoning that if she could keep her feet from going to sleep the rest of her would oblige and stay awake. She suppressed a shiver; as well as boots, she was wearing leggings, three-quarter-length trousers, a T-shirt, a long-sleeved top and a blanket as a wrap, and it still felt the wrong side of cold in her office. GlimpseCorp economised on heating and air conditioning in its lower offices; also on carpets, windows and furniture.

McHugh was in his early sixties, but he had the look of someone who still expected the world to deliver on its promises. Shikha studied him with a mixture of pity and envy. If the Glimpse Show taught you anything, it was that the world is much more likely to dangle its promises in front of you long enough to get your attention then snatch them away and laugh in your face. But there was no telling some people. These people. The people waiting outside her door. All desperate for the fame and money that the Glimpse Show offered. There was no telling them.

For their first interview, they were channelled through a basement back door in the GlimpseCorp tower building and made to stand for hours in stuffy, dimly lit hallways, all the while being subjected to electronic music on a loop—a short loop—and when their moment arrived at last and they reached the head of the queue, they got to talk to lowly employees like Shikha. And all that tedium didn't put them off. On the contrary, it made them think that their efforts and determination were hard-won.

The trouble was that people looked at the soaring glamour of the GlimpseCorp tower and they forgot the standing and the waiting and the terrible music, because they thought what they could hear was the click of high heels on marble floors, the swish of silk-lined suits, and the clink of ice cubes in crystal glasses; they imagined themselves there, chosen for the Show.

Shikha wanted to say to the man sitting opposite her, *Go home, Mr McHugh. Go home to your wife or your drinking buddies or your dog, because this glimpse of yours is next to useless.*

'Honest to God,' he was now saying, 'they're as real as the hand in front of my face.' He chuckled and exhibited a large, hairy hand as evidence.

She found that she could not smile back.

'Right, then,' said McHugh. 'You put my name down there, missy, and you get me on that show.' He laced his fingers across his paunch and sat back, nodding at the memory of his glimpses, his shot at stardom.

'How do you feel when they happen?' she asked.

'Eh?' He shifted backwards in his chair as though she had offered him a cup of mouse tea.

'Do you feel happy or sad or scared or overwhelmed… anything like that?'

'This part of the test?'

'It's not a test, sir. The tests come later, if you are selected for the next round of interviews.'

He shifted again and gazed at the ceiling. The tiles were grey with accumulated breath and evaporated sweat. No answers were written on them. 'I guess,' said Mr McHugh, staring hard, 'I guess I feel…happy?' He grabbed at the word and darted a look at her.

Liar, she thought. 'And do your glimpses come with every quake?'

'Oh, yes. They sure do.'

Again, doubtful. To experience a glimpse with every single quake? You'd be a basket case very quickly. Most genuine glimpsers seemed to get them—or to notice them—with the bigger quakes, not the little shakes that happened throughout each day.

'Thank you, Mr McHugh.' She leaned forward a fraction, with a nod and a smile, and closed her tablet gently. 'You'll be hearing from us.'

The next three candidates were, first, a young woman who thought she saw a tree or perhaps it was a power pole, then a kid whose mates had dared him to make up a glimpse so pornographic he'd get thrown out before he got halfway through it, which duly happened, and finally a man who began with, 'Well, it's usually real dark.'

Shikha finished work at 4 pm because the delightful prospect of spending two hours at the night market in the D-Zone awaited her. She had nothing to show for her day's work at the GlimpseCorp tower, and knew for certain that she'd have nothing to show for tonight's mind-numbing stretch in the D-Zone either. Those two last night, Jonah and Evie, had made that very clear.

Shikha pushed her fingers through her hair and massaged her scalp. She felt a headache coming on, which was just what she needed. She was fed up with her lowly job. Stuck in the basement being polite to people she'd never met before and would never meet again, who saw her as the lowest rung on a ladder to their dreams of fame. Minimum wage. No perks. No benefits. She was fairly certain that no one in the thirty-nine floors above her knew her name. Or respected the fact that she was diligent about her job. She wondered if the reason they sent security with her to the D-Zone was to make sure she actually went there instead of skiving off. She would have skived off tonight if she hadn't had her guard in tow. She told herself that at least she had a front-row seat for the unfolding wonder of the holo light show, and not many people had that. But it wasn't helping her find recruits. The attractions of the Glimpse Show, it seemed, were no match for the promises PANN was making to glimpsers—that glimpsing was an essential, indeed mystical, part of this whole new-world schtick.

She locked her tablet away as though it held a store of precious data from her day's interviews, instead of nothing worth a bean. A worry was creeping up on her, had been for a while: that what she was seeing with her would-be recruits was not an aberration but a trend.

The glimpses were fading.

The accounts she was hearing now were like shadows of the glimpses people had reported to her in the past. They'd become blurred somehow, as though glimpsers were peering at them through thick, smudged lenses.

If the glimpses were fading, would they soon disappear? That was a terrifying thought. It meant the end of the Glimpse Show, but that wasn't the terrifying bit. Without glimpsing, there could be no quake warning system.

The system had sprung up in the early quake days in neighbourhoods across the city as people realised they had glimpsers in their midst. When it became clear that glimpsing was widespread, City Hall had instituted a warning system in which glimpsers were rostered to various parts of the city to set the alarms ringing when a quake was on the way. There had been a big drop in casualties since then and glimpsers had been elevated to superhero status. The quakes were still frightening and damaging, of course, but they had become much more survivable.

Shikha sat hunched against the cold in her GlimpseCorp stall. Her minder had gone for a walk among the holos. For once, she wished he'd stayed with her. The atmosphere in Linden Plaza had darkened in recent days and she had become nervous being alone in her stall. PANN had saturated the plaza, and beyond for all she knew, with pamphlets and posters proclaiming the coming of a New Nation. Bands of PANN followers roamed about with their collection bags, encouraging people to donate. The big anniversary was only ten days away now and it was clear from their spiel that if you wanted to be in on the great transformation, then you needed to pay up.

Earlier in the evening, the gospel choir had given a mini-concert on the church steps. Shikha stood up to watch and found herself swaying with the rhythm of the old songs like 'Peace in the Valley' and 'Down in the River to Pray'. Evie lifted her rich, jazzy alto easily across the plaza. A boy, maybe ten years old, sang beside her, his voice a sweet soprano. Here was a more peaceful soundtrack for the D-Zone than the urgent, haunting saxophone that regularly poured out of the church demanding everyone's attention.

Shikha was puzzled that few in the crowd stopped in front of the choir, or swayed or danced to those gentle songs. Most passed by nervously, not looking at the singers, and there was only a scatter of applause after each song. At the end of the last song, the pastor, who was also the choir conductor, stepped up to the microphone. He was a tall man with hair greying at the temples and a distinguished bearing. He thanked the crowd. Then he said, 'Remember, folks, God doesn't need your money. He asks only for mercy and justice and love. We've done it tough these last few years, that's true. But paying out your hard-earned cash for a fantasy won't make it come true. The Lord says, *Beware the false prophets who come to you in sheep's clothing. Inwardly they are ravening wolves.*' He held up a hand in blessing. 'Bless you. Peace to you all.'

With the choir packed up and gone, and her minder off seeing the sights, Shikha was thinking about button-holing passers-by to ask them directly whether they glimpsed, when Bas, who used to work at Nemy's Stuffed Potatoes rushed up to the pizza stand. Jonah glanced at him but kept working. Bas leaned close to the counter and was talking quiet and fast—Shikha couldn't make out what he was saying without being obvious in her eavesdropping. Jonah said something that made Bas take a step back and as he did so, a young man in PANN blue with bleached hair cropped short marched up and stood beside him. Shikha knocked a stack of her own pamphlets off her table so that she could come out of her stall to pick them up and get within earshot. Jonah was putting on his polite face to the newcomer. 'What can I get for you? Specials are right there on the board. I recommend—'

'I'm issuing your business a non-compliance notice,' said the man. 'His too.' He nodded towards Nemy's Stuffed Potatoes, which was closed tonight because Nemy hadn't taken on a replacement for Bas.

Jonah looked pointedly at Bas then back at the newcomer. 'Yeah? What gives you the right to do that?'

The man leaned in and gripped Jonah's wrist. Shikha stood up, pamphlets in hand, wondering if she should yell for help.

The man said to Jonah, 'People are about to learn exactly which businesses are welcoming of our great purpose and which are stuck in unbelief.'

Jonah wrenched his arm free. 'Try it. See how far you get.' He glared at Bas and said, 'Are you cool with this?'

Bas opened his mouth to reply but Jonah said, 'Forget it. Go and play with your new buddies.'

Bas turned his back and left.

The man reached up and slapped a large sticker with a blue background and a black X on the pizza stall's canopy; he did the same to Nemy's stall, then he turned and pointed at Jonah. 'Ten days!' he said and marched away.

Jonah came away from his counter to scrape at the sticker, swearing under his breath.

'You okay?' Shikha ventured out from her stall. 'That was crazy.'

Jonah looked across at her and smiled. 'Yeah, course. No one around here pays any mind to patsy warnings like that. Unless it's from our gangland overlords, of course. Them, we watch out for. I'm not gonna fold on a threat like that. Art's customers keep coming back because his pizzas are great.'

'Your pizzas now. I haven't seen Art for a while.'

Jonah shrugged. 'He'll be back. This will all blow over.'

'Do you think that will be anytime soon?'

He grimaced. 'I hope so? Is that wishful thinking?'

'They're pompous, aren't they, with their Great Purpose and their fancy blue and white colour scheme.' She picked up a poster that had been scuffed on the pavement and studied it. 'Do you know anything about this new nation?'

Jonah dumped the scraped-off sticker in his bin and wiped his hands. He leaned on his counter, watching the man who'd just threatened him work the crowd, Bas trailing behind him. He turned back to Shikha. 'They're telling people that the D-Zone is ground zero for some kind of reinvented city, or nation, and that it's all gonna kick off on the seventh anniversary of the first quake in, like he said, ten days' time. Apparently, a massive quake will cut us off from everywhere else and we'll make a new nation here with our own government and our own laws.' He raised his eyebrows. 'Sounds likely, doesn't it! But it appeals to some people, as you can tell.' He waved an arm at the crowd, where PANN followers were in happy, animated conversation with locals.

'I've even seen a couple of the gang bosses mooching around here. They were pretending to check out the holos, but I bet they were talking to Phaedra and Damon about whether to back them or not. I don't know how that'll go because those guys don't play well together, and they don't play second fiddle to anyone, so I can't see them working for someone else's Great Purpose.

'And, anyway, you can bet that when PANN says "Let's make our own laws" they mean they'll make the laws and the rest of us will follow them.' He smiled without pleasure. 'Like the gangs are gonna stand for that.' He took some money from a customer and nodded his thanks. 'And then,' he went on, 'there's some mumbo jumbo about the holos coming to life because the new nation will, who knows, maybe change the laws of nature as well. It's all bull. They just want money, and when they've bled us dry they'll up and leave again. And I hope they take their light show with them.'

'You really don't like them.'

Jonah watched one of them wander past then his eyes skimmed the crowd and she wondered if he was looking for his friend. 'I really don't,' he said. 'They're riling people up and dividing the place between believers and unbelievers. You heard that guy? So, I'm stuck in unbelief. I'm not the only one, but we're a target now. They hit the Matterhorn—that's where we live—a few days ago with a brick through a window. And someone's had a go with some spray paint so we've got graffiti too.'

'Oh, no. That's awful.'

'Yeah. We can paint it over. It's no big deal.'

'JONAH! JONAH!' The kid from the choir came barrelling up at speed and almost collided with the pizza stall.

'Mikey!' said Jonah. 'What's going on?'

'A…a…a…' The kid put his hands on his knees, gasping, and when he stood up Shikha realised he was not just breathless, but crying.

'Hey, now,' she said, 'Breathe. Take your time.'

'A fire!' said the kid. 'At home! Someone threw a…a…a…'

'A what?' demanded Jonah. He was ripping off his apron.

'Something—I don't know—through the window and it blew up and— Can you come?'

'You bet!' Jonah looked at his oven and then at Shikha. 'Can you watch the oven for me? It has to cool down before I can close up. I'll be back.'

The glowing embers of the wood-fired oven were a lot more inviting than her own cold stall. Shikha said, 'Of course! Of course. You go.'

'Sorry! Thanks!'

'Go!'

He was already running, Mikey panting at his heels.

Shikha's minder was not pleased. 'We can't babysit some guy's stall. Who knows when he'll be back?'

'It's an emergency.'

'Yeah, well, I've got an emergency appointment with my couch and a beer tonight and I'm not going to be late for it, okay?' He looked at his watch. 'It's closing time.'

It was, but Shikha had no intention of leaving. This was her chance, at last, to get in with these people. If she left now, her one contact here would drop her because she'd betrayed his trust and she'd never break her drought in this place. And then she might as well kiss her career progression at GlimpseCorp goodbye.

The minder had started packing up the stall.

Shikha said, 'I'll find my own way home.'

He glanced at her and went back to packing up.

'Don't be stupid. What if—'

'What if I get attacked on the way? Here,' she fumbled in one of the boxes for a pen and a scrap of paper. 'Let me write you a note, absolving you of all blame if I turn up dead on a D-Zone street tomorrow.'

He finished packing, stood up and scowled at her.

She held out the note she'd scrawled. 'Now, go. Please.'

He took it, read it, hesitated for slightly longer than she'd expected, then sloped off, looking back at her a few times and grumbling.

She watched him go and muttered, 'Good riddance.' Then she packed up the rest of her own things and went to sit in the warmth emanating from Jonah's pizza oven.

Time ticked on. Shikha waited and watched as other stall holders packed up and left. The crowd thinned. She pulled her hat down over her ears again, rewrapped her scarf, and tried not to think what it would be like to spend the night here, alone with this forest of the dead.

The embers were grey by the time Jonah came racing back to her. 'Sorry!' he said. 'Thank you so much.'

'What's happened?'

He shook his head. 'It's bad. An explosive through a window. It got Evie's dad. He's hurt. I don't know how much. They've taken him to a clinic.' He pushed his fingers through his hair. 'I don't know—how did it get out of control so quick? I mean, people know Evie's dad. They like him! Who would do this?' He checked his watch. 'Shit. It's nearly midnight. I'm sorry—you didn't need to get caught up in this. What do you want to do? We could try calling a cab but to be honest, no-one's coming this far east this time of night. I could…' he hesitated. 'Do you want to come home to the Matterhorn? We've got a spare room you could camp in. I dunno—you hardly know us. But we're your safest bet right now.'

'Don't panic,' said Shikha. 'It's fine. I'll come back with you.'

He looked surprised and relieved that she was so ready to dive into the unknown. 'Okay, cool. Let's go then.'

Darkness crept out from the buildings on each side of the road as Shikha and Jonah hurried away from the plaza, Jonah wheeling his bike and Shikha striding beside him, trying to look confident. After ten minutes, she was having doubts about her decision to do this. The wind was howling down dark alleys and the sky began to spit sleet. Now and then they passed a glowing street brazier with people huddled round it. Shikha could feel the scrutiny of everyone they passed as though she was carrying a sign declaring her Not a Local.

She pulled her hat round her ears and her collar round her face. Someone behind her laughed and she spun round but it was just two people across the road calling goodnight to each other, then a dog barked and Shikha jumped again but it was answered by another bark and someone yelling, 'Quiet, ya mongrel!' And on it went. She jumped at noises, shadows, lights, movement, the wind and the rain.

Jonah didn't speak the whole way, although every minute or so he looked across at her as if he was checking that she hadn't been snatched from his side and dragged off into the night. She realised, on reflection, why. D-Zone inhabitants were watchful. They watched where they walked so they didn't twist ankles on the broken streets, and they watched what they walked under because a big tremor could peel the side off a building or drop an awning. Also, they watched to see whose turf they were on and then they watched their backs.

Her nerves were stretched so tight by the time Jonah stopped she thought the brightly lit oasis in front of her must be a mirage. It was a sprawling weatherboard building with multi-paned windows lit with warm yellow light and a veranda lined with chairs to catch the afternoon sun. It was like finding a diamond in a puddle.

She could see graffiti sprayed across the big bay window. It was hard to decipher but it could have said 'SCUM'. There was no sign of a fire.

'I thought—' began Shikha. 'The fire?'

'Round the other side,' said Jonah. 'They knew where to throw it. Through the study window. Evie's dad was the only one in there, thank goodness.'

'No one else hurt?'

'No. Other people were here and put it out.' Jonah frowned. 'Everything's gone up a whole new level. We need to get everyone in the choir to somewhere safe, that's for sure. People think they're anti-PANN.' He paused. 'Well, they are, but since when was it a crime to disagree with stupid?'

They were still standing outside and Shikha was visibly shivering.

'Sorry!' said Jonah. 'Come in.'

He led her inside to a warm kitchen and gave her a bowl of soup. And then he paced, until Evie came back.

'Of course you have to leave,' Jonah was saying to Evie. 'You can't stay here. None of you can. At least till after the anniversary.'

'No way,' said Evie. She was lit up from inside, restless, eyes fiery. Her father was badly hurt. Burns. Concussion. Even some kind of shrapnel that had been in the device and had buried itself in his flesh. He might lose an eye. Evie had been distraught when she got home and had held on to Jonah and sobbed for a long while. Now she was angry.

Shikha glanced at Jonah. He was following every word, watching Evie with frowning intent—there was such worry and such sweetness there, it made her heart ache. She thought that he would sit and watch Evie talk about anything, or not talk, it wouldn't matter—that he'd do that for hours. He was looking desperate now.

'Please—' he began.

Evie stopped in front of him, put a finger on his lips and kissed his forehead. 'I'm not leaving. We fight on. We challenge this anniversary B-S. Also, I need to be near my dad in case…in case…' Her eyes welled with tears for a moment, but she quelled them with a deep breath and resumed her restless movement around the kitchen.

'Jesus, Evie,' Jonah shook his head, defeated. 'They're not gonna stop.'

Shikha stirred. 'Is there anything I can do?'

'No,' said Evie, turning to her. 'Thank you.'

But Jonah said, 'Yes. There is something.'

Evie stopped and looked at him.

'I want to go on your show,' he said to Shikha. 'I want people to know what PANN really is.'

Shikha frowned at him. 'But you have to be able to glimpse to go on the show.'

'I know,' said Jonah. 'Your lucky day.'

8

'BUT WHY DIDN'T you tell me before?' asked Shikha.

'Well,' said Jonah, 'there's a problem.'

The problem was Jonah's citizenship papers: he didn't have any. Typical, thought Shikha. She'd finally found someone who could glimpse, really glimpse. Jonah told her what he saw and she had been amazed at the amount of detail. Finally! Gold! And almost within reach. And now, he wasn't eligible because he had no damn papers.

'Wouldn't they make an exception?' he asked.

She shook her head. 'No. And wouldn't you be crazy to want them to? Like you kept telling me, you might as well knock on the door at Border Control and hand yourself in.' She sighed and frowned, thinking. 'Although…'

'What?' he asked.

'If they want you badly enough they might not look too closely.'

He sat back. 'Forged papers.'

She grimaced. 'Well… I know they're desperate for some good, clear, authentic glimpsing. And you fit the bill. I think maybe they'd be so keen that they wouldn't notice? But I don't have the first idea how to go about it.'

Jonah nodded. 'I do. Only thing is, it's pricey.'

'Oh. Okay. How pricey?'

'Let's find out.'

Jonah put his shoulder to the large door of the baroque old building he'd led Shikha to and smiled at her as he pushed it open. 'Welcome,' he said, 'to Hotel Dirac.' He walked inside and she hesitated then followed. A gust of dead leaves blew in with them and skittered across the atrium's cracked mosaic floor. Shikha stood still and gazed around her.

Five storeys above them the empty frames of skylights slanted sunshine into the ghost-gloomy light below. Their shattered glass had mostly been swept into piles in the corners. A vast staircase at the northern end of the atrium zigzagged up towards the roof. You could step off at each of the levels and walk down internal balconies of wrought iron and once-polished wooden bannisters.

'Oh,' she breathed, because Hotel Dirac was, or was once, splendid.

They'd come here hoping for the papers that Jonah needed to go on the Glimpse Show. Shikha had said she would find the money to pay for them, but first they needed to know how much money they were talking about. So here they were, standing in the midst of this ruined grandeur.

After the first big quakes, once people had picked themselves up, dusted themselves off and looked around at their newly broken cityscape, the decision had been made to draw a line separating Things Not Worth Repairing from Things that Must be Repaired as Soon as Possible. That line ran along the edge of Wulfstan Wood, and around the D-Zone, demarcating it from anything that might be called The ReBuild, Progress and/or Going Forward. Hotel Dirac sat on the border of the Wood, on the wrong side of the line.

Jonah's torch cast a small pool of light, but it was so meagre that instead of dispelling the darkness it made the shadows deeper. Shikha stood close to him peering into the gloom and having second thoughts.

'Lift's out,' said a voice.

Shikha jumped and swore.

'Chance!' said Jonah and walked towards a dark corner.

Shikha saw the flare of a cigarette being lit. 'Wait!' she followed him. 'What are you doing?'

'It's okay,' said Jonah. 'It's Last Chance Jackson.'

'I called Maintenance,' the voice went on.

'Oh, yeah?' said Jonah as they arrived in a corner where a man with thinning white hair and a sparse beard drew on a cigarette from the depths of a dilapidated armchair. A sleeping bag lay beside him and from its folds a ginger cat emerged, then purred around Jonah's ankles. He scooped her up. 'And what did Maintenance say?'

The man blew out a plume of smoke pungent enough to make Shikha gag. He grinned. 'Jonah, my lad, they said they'd be round just as soon as they'd sourced a new supply of cocktail umbrellas and clean towels.'

Jonah nodded and put the cat down. 'Thought as much. What the hell are you smoking?'

The man peered at the lit end of his rollie. 'Nothing good. I'd offer you one but…'

'Yeah. You want to keep your friends. Alphonsine here?'

The man's eyes narrowed. 'I believe so.' He looked at Shikha enquiringly.

'Oh,' said Jonah. 'This is Shikha. She's from Over There.'

'Greetings, Shikha from Over There.'

She smiled nervously.

'Social call?' he asked.

Jonah smiled and didn't say.

The man waved his cigarette towards the staircase.

'You'll have to take the stairs. And Jonah…'

'Yup?'

'If you're playing with the big guns, mind how you go.'

'Sure, Chance. Thanks.'

A stiff climb later, they walked along the fifth-level balcony to a massive door. Jonah knocked and Shikha peered over the balcony. The sense of space above, below and all around her was tremendous. They were near the skylights, but the clouds had darkened and it wasn't much brighter here than it had been below. The door opened.

'My angel!' The woman named Alphonsine greeted Jonah with arms thrown wide. 'Where have you been? Your old auntie has missed you. Come in, come in.' She ushered them inside with a smile at Shikha. 'I have made a pot of rose pouchong tea. I must have known you were coming. Come! Come!' She led them into a large room with a high ceiling with elaborate plaster mouldings. Dim daylight entered through two tall sets of windows and cast itself like dusk across the space.

Shikha nudged Jonah. 'You didn't say she was your aunt.'

'She's not,' said Jonah.

They sat on a couch the colour of shadow and watched as the tea was put down before them. 'In your honour,' said Alphonsine, 'we will have light.' She went around the room lighting candles, some thick as an elephant's leg, some tall and slender set in elaborate candelabra.

Shikha watched her, wondering how old she was. It was hard to tell. She wore her great length of shining black hair pinned up by a silver clasp with a giant blue bead. She was wrapped in bright florals with large gemstones—maybe real, maybe not—on long loops around her neck; her lips were red, her eyes kohled, her profile regal with a very straight nose and high forehead.

Rain had begun falling outside the windows, but the room was warm and the tea was sweet and soothing. Jonah and Alphonsine exchanged quake news the way people talk about the weather.

'Anything broken?' asked Jonah. The quake this morning had been a rolling beast that had Shikha nauseous and wondering if it would ever stop. They'd all been at breakfast when Jonah's glimpse arrived and she had watched fascinated and slightly horrified as he sat forward, elbows on knees, head in hands, a faint cry from his lips. The glimpse had lasted maybe ten seconds. Long enough. Then he sat up and blew out a sharp breath. He didn't need to tell people what was coming. They scattered to warn others. Someone banged a gong on the veranda, then the quake arrived and rolled for the best part of a minute.

'Broken?' Alphonsine's laugh was deep. 'No, child,

there is nothing here left to break.' Shikha was fairly certain that this was untrue. For a start, there was the china tea set they were sipping from. Then there were all the strange treasures that filled the room: antique maps on the walls, a polished brass telescope, a miniature wooden rocking horse, a cabinet with dozens of tiny drawers, a small statue of a martial-arts figure waving a curved sword. They were things that might have come from a junk shop three blocks away but might also have been retrieved from ancient palaces in faraway countries.

Shikha sipped her tea and ate a small, perfectly formed shell of shortbread.

'I need help,' said Jonah.

Alphonsine lifted one magnificent eyebrow.

'Papers.'

Alphonsine replaced her cup in its saucer with exquisite care and the warm, auntie vibe slipped from her like a discarded cloak. 'Why?'

She listened as Jonah explained.

When he'd finished, she said, 'First. You know how dangerous it is to be caught with forged papers.' The woman looked at Shikha. 'Worse than no papers. Second.' She looked back at Jonah. 'You have no evidence of wrongdoing by PANN. What is the worth of your word against theirs?'

'There's other people out there who've been scammed,' said Jonah. 'This needs to get out and be talked about.

They *steal* from people. They ruin people's lives.'

Alphonsine studied him. 'They hurt you and your family—'

'And their followers hurt Evie and her family. I have to do something. I have to. I hate them.'

'Revenge is a poor rationale.'

He was silent for a second. Then he said, 'It's not revenge. Or not only. I just want a chance…' He stopped.

A chance at redemption, thought Shikha. At setting something right to make up for the mistake he made, the damage he caused, all those years ago when he believed in PANN's promises.

Jonah went on, 'Someone's going to get killed soon. Evie's dad nearly was. I know what they are and if I sit by and let that happen, it'll be my fault.'

Alphonsine considered him for a long time. 'I will help you this much.' She glanced at Shikha. 'My papers are the best, but even they will not withstand full BCB scrutiny. They can, however, be used for most other purposes. But'—she sighed—'we do what we can.' She turned back to Jonah. 'I will give you temporary papers. That way if you are caught with them by the BCB you can claim to be In Process and they may not bother to check. But these papers expire in six weeks. Is that time enough?'

Shikha said, 'I'll make sure of it.' But she spoke with more certainty than she felt. She'd need to get him on the current season of the show, which would mean bumping someone else. It was worth a go. 'And the price?'

Alphonsine named a fee that was not as eye-watering as Shikha had feared. 'All right,' she said. 'We can manage that.'

'I'll pay you back,' said Jonah.

Alphonsine stood up. 'Come back in two days.'

9

SHIKHA WAS PART of GlimpseCorp's frontline, dealing with the onrush of eager and ambitious glimpsers who hoped to find fame on the Glimpse Show. Glimpses came to people strobe-like in a kaleidoscope of visions, sometimes flickering on the edge of consciousness, sometimes flooding the senses and overwhelming the glimpser. It was Shikha's job to sift gold-dust from sawdust among the applicants, finding fragments in the glimpses of the chosen few that could be drawn out, detail by detail, so that her glimpsers could build clear accounts to take into the show.

Filmed in front of a hysterically eager audience, the show was beamed live to a country craving a sugar rush to escape the existential threat of disappearing in the next big quake. The pearl at its heart was the fact that glimpses were genuine predictors of earthquakes. The genius of the show's creators was to morph this strange gift into a genre-defying phenomenon. Glimpsers were hailed, variously, as heroes for predicting quakes, as mutants ushering in the next stage in human evolution, as 'earth whisperers' in touch with the growing pains of the planet, and as PTSD victims, hypersensitive to quakes, who could use their affliction to save lives. No one could prove any of it, of course, which left the field wide open for all kinds of crazy.

Guests became instant celebrities. Being on the show opened doors to breakfast TV, afternoon soaps and evening game shows and, of course, to opportunities for product endorsements and money, money, money.

By the time these would-be celebrities walked into the spotlight and sat on the famous blue couch with show hosts Brett and Bev, their accounts of fragmentary glimpses had become simple, clear and dramatic—not at all the chaotic experiences that they had first related to the likes of Shikha. Complexity was not welcome on the Glimpse Show; it was shushed and shown the door well before the party kicked off.

The GlimpseCorp SFX studios reconstructed the glimpses into short films, and Brett and Bev led each guest through their history of glimpsing: what they saw, where they'd first glimpsed, where they'd recently glimpsed, the quakes they'd predicted and the lives they'd saved. Life stories were told and interrogated while scientists, psychics, theologians and the occasional philosopher weighed in.

At the emotional heart of each show Brett and Bev accompanied a glimpser to the site of their most significant glimpse and interviewed people who'd been saved from injury and even death by the warning. Dr Zac, the show's resident psychologist, explained why each person had had this glimpse in this place at this time in their lives. Histories were uncovered, revelations ensued.

The show had been a goldmine for GlimpseCorp. But as glimpsing began to fade so the gold began to disappear and the show could not survive that.

Shikha made it home to her bedsit before dark the night after her adventure in the D-Zone. She made herself a comforting bowl of noodles in a broth of lemongrass, ginger, red curry and coconut milk and settled to watch tonight's show.

One of her gulls, Julia, was appearing. She got into trouble calling them gulls, but it suited them well. They were so hungry. They wanted so much, and they'd believe anything that convinced them they were on an upward track to fame and fortune.

From their first interview, Shikha had liked Julia's glimpse: purple hills in a half light.

'It's quiet here,' said Julia, in a voice-over to her recreated glimpse. 'I can hear myself breathe.' She couldn't but what was a little fabrication between friends? 'I'm on a hillside. There's a carpet of tiny white flowers where I'm standing, and behind me are more hills, layers of them; they're turning different shades of blue and purple in the setting sun. I can feel the emptiness of this place…'

Julia's sunset glimpse provided a gentle early-season episode. The producers of the show liked to build through the season towards more spectacular fare later on. Future episodes were trailed at the end of tonight's show. There was Benjamin's storm at sea: in his glimpse video, he stood teetering on rocks at the sea's edge, buffeted by wild winds and the spray from waves that crashed gigantically onto the shore below. His glimpse would give Dr Zac a chance to search for and find sufficient trauma in Ben's childhood to offer a highly dubious but sensational interpretation of his glimpsing and thereby keep the ratings buoyant for another week.

There was Tomasita, the intellectual of the season, a tiny young woman with direct brown eyes and curious, upstanding red hair. In her glimpse, she sat cross-legged beside a campfire on a vast empty plain with the glory of the night sky washing over her and snow-covered mountains in the faraway. Her episode was intended to convey that 'hey, we're not just about exploiting trauma and manipulating emotions—there are existential questions at stake here too.' Philosophers and theologians would be invited to weigh in on that episode.

In the season finale, there would be Audri, of the auburn hair and ivory skin, draped around a tree in a forest, haughty as an elf queen, with a black panther crouching at her bare bejewelled feet and a pout so perfect it deserved its own name. Shikha knew the panther was wildly unlikely—a lot of people thought so and said so at length wherever comment was free—but Audri had aced the lie detector in her audition so either she was delusional on a grand scale (very likely, thought Shikha) or she genuinely had seen a panther in a forest.

The season was already in full swing and each episode, though broadcast live, was carefully planned in advance. Shikha had imagined how Jonah's episode would go and she was certain it was a winner. The fact that she wouldn't have any say in it didn't stop her from seeing it all in her head.

It would be about growing up in the D-Zone, living among that desolation, losing his parents, not to death but to the consequences of the quakes that so many people lived with daily but which were mostly invisible. A film crew would go there: it would marvel at the beauty and sorrow of the hologram shrine, it would interview people saved by Jonah's glimpses, it would show D-Zone life in its raw state and, at its climax, Jonah would confront the PANN siblings, Phaedra and Damon, and expose them for blighting his childhood with a con that everyone would condemn.

This, Shikha was sure, would be an easy sell to the GlimpseCorp higher-ups; she just had to work out how to ask them for money without telling them it was to pay for Jonah's papers. She had agonised over how much she should tell them and decided that she would simply say that, because he was a poverty-stricken boy from the Zone, he needed an advance for the time he had to take off work to prep for the show and that he was prepared to sign on any dotted line to promise to pay it all back. In most circumstances, she thought, the higher-ups would not countenance this, but his story was so good, how could they turn him down?

In the morning, Shikha headed into work, excited for the first time in a long time about how her day would go.

10

THIRTY-NINE FLOORS ABOVE Shikha's basement office, Kerryn Duval, the head of Glimpse Corporation, stood at a panoramic window and watched the rain-clouded city slide towards dusk. Behind her, an impeccably tidy glass-topped desk reflected her trim silhouette—the immaculate suit and smooth bob cut. In front of the desk a dishevelled-looking man was fidgeting. He had been up for twenty-three hours, wading through data in the hope that he wouldn't end up standing exactly where he was now, saying exactly what he'd just said.

Duval did not look at him, which he felt to be a mercy.

'We know this, Dr Fisher.' She lifted her hands in exasperation. 'We've known it for some time. I don't really care about the why. What I need to know is—how quickly?'

He put his hands behind his back. 'In some places, ah, locally in the east, that is, there still seems to be a profusion of glimpsing, although it's hard to get good data there. The indications from all our sources—our crowd mapping, our people in the field, our surveys, our auditions for the Show, our psych assessments—'

The woman turned around and he took an involuntary step backwards.

'I'm not doubting you,' she said. 'Is this a temporary hiatus, or a permanent decline?'

'It's impossible to say, Ms Duval.'

Her eyebrows lifted. 'That's a pity, isn't it. Because it's worth a great deal to us to know one way or the other. I don't want the markets to know before we do that the glimpses are definitely disappearing—if that is the case. There are share prices and shareholders to think about. I'm sure you understand?'

'We're working hard on it. We need time to track the trends. But I should have something more definitive for you within the month.'

'A month. I see.' Now she was frowning. 'That's far too long.'

'I'm sorry, ma'am. It's the nature of the data and—'

Duval stepped back to her desk, already examining tomorrow's schedule. 'Two weeks, Dr Fisher. Earlier would be better, obviously.' She waved a hand dismissing him.

Instinctively, he started to bow but noticed in time and fled.

She watched the door close then, still not raising her voice, she said, 'Morgan. In here, please.'

A door next to her bookcase opened and a man slipped into the room. He was a thin, long-legged man with a pale face and light brown hair slicked back from a high forehead. He was wearing a dark blue suit, an unfortunate choice on one level because it emphasised the sallow cast of his skin. But on another level, it worked for him; he was a man who knew his task was not to shine, but to slip unnoticed through doors and crowds, gathering information and bestowing it as necessary in a manner that ensured he was consistently underestimated.

Kerryn Duval was still studying her schedule. 'What do you think?'

Morgan sat down in a chair meant for visitors, leaned back and steepled his fingers. 'I think we need a change of strategy.'

'Obviously. Feel free…'

'As you wish. We'll have to pivot. Chase down some tragic quake stories, perhaps? Follow up our former show guests to see if celebrity has destroyed their lives? That kind of thing.'

She almost smiled. 'Oh, please. You think too small. We have a show that even I'm bored with, on a channel that's run out of ideas, focused entirely on a phenomenon that appears to be rapidly disappearing. And we have Jericho snapping at our heels.' Jericho. The opposition.

Bright young things who were prepared to take outrageous risks to win the ratings war. She turned her back on Morgan and gazed out at the darkening afternoon. 'I have an idea.'

Morgan pursed his lips. 'I thought you might. Not one for sharing with the board, I imagine?'

She turned back to him. 'Yesterday's men. I saw this coming months ago. I've been working on a plan for some time.'

'A plan! My word! How bold. And you didn't tell me?'

Her gaze hardened. 'And I'm not telling you now either. I just wanted your take on the Fade, as we might call it. In the meantime, why do I have this?' She waved a piece of paper at him, holding it away from her between thumb and forefinger, as though it was unclean.

He leaned forward. 'If I may?' He took it and read it, eyebrows raised.

'Why do I,' she went on, 'have to deal with every little detail of running this company? Every. Little. Detail. This appears to be a request for money for a Show participant. I don't know how it ended up on my desk—some foolish underling obviously thought I should see it. What on earth?'

Morgan frowned. 'A participant from the D-Zone. We haven't had one of those before. This could be good, you know. The person making the request,' he looked again at the paper, 'Shikha Doran, she's been over in the D-Zone almost daily for six months trying to recruit glimpsers.'

'Well, at last. It's taken long enough. Why is it costing us money?'

'I will investigate.'

11

A MAN NAMED Morgan from the 39th floor sent for Shikha—the same man who had consigned her, many months ago, to the stall at the D-Zone night market. Her instructions then had been few. Find some glimpsers from that wretched place. He'd told her it would be easy. 'Glimpsing for money and glory. That's all they need to know. That's all they'll be interested in. Just get on with it.'

Now, at last, she had found someone. The man regarded her with dead-fish eyes and introduced himself as Mr Morgan; he'd assumed she'd forgotten him. He had almost certainly forgotten her.

He slapped a piece of paper down on his desk. 'Explain, please.'

She picked it up and he said, 'Well?'

'Ah,' Shikha swallowed. 'It's all here. It's just an

advance on future earnings from being on the show. If Jonah takes time out from his pizza stall he has no income. He's the only one I've been able to find over there. And his glimpse is remarkable. It's—'

'Not important. You've left it too late. He can audition for our next season.' Morgan was already waving her out the door.

Shikha was ready for this. 'But what if the holo-field is gone by then? PANN probably won't be there past the seventh anniversary and that's only a week away. And if we want to capture the holos and PANN in the show, we should get him on straightaway. We could make it an anniversary special and do it actually on the seventh anniversary.'

Morgan studied her with the dead-fish eyes. 'A director now, are you?'

Shikha blushed. 'There's so much we could put in this episode. I've been there all these weeks and I've got lots of ideas—'

He held up a hand. 'I'm sure you do.' He paused, narrowing his eyes at her. 'We don't have the budget for an extra episode, but the anniversary is a drawcard, that's true. I'll think about it. As for the advance, I'll think about that too.'

'I'll stand security for it.'

His eyebrows shot up. 'Why?'

Why, indeed? It was two months' wages.

'Because,' she lifted her chin. 'I trust Jonah. And I think this episode could be sensational. He'll have lots of offers out of it.' And she would be the one who'd made it happen. She would be noticed at last. And from that, she could apply to be an assistant on the show. One day she would be a director and she would smile down at Morgan from those lofty heights and ask him to bring her coffee.

Morgan was looking amused. 'All right. I'll send you the paperwork for the loan. Make sure you sign it.'

Back in the basement, Shikha picked up her phone and checked her bank balance; she didn't need to—she knew exactly how close she was skating to the edge. The edge was always close and she was adept at skating alongside it. Whenever she was tempted by a luxury like a cab or a movie, she peered over it and got a salutary attack of vertigo. But Morgan had said he'd consider her idea. This was a chance, an amazing chance. She felt as though a rope ladder had been unfurled from a balloon sailing high and handsome above this quake-rotten city and she was about to lift off and sail into her own brilliant future.

12

THE VIEW WAS sensational. Jonah wished Evie was here to see it. He was on the 15th floor of the Glimpse Corporation building gazing at the cityscape where dozens of towering cranes were bending and pecking at the rebuild. In the square directly below, everything was as tidy as a grandmother's living room: rows of trees inside low, trimmed hedges, the brightly lit windows of fancy boutiques. No rubbish was blowing about, and no streeties lounged in shop doorways. Even the slanting afternoon sunlight on the snow-swept borders looked stage-managed.

People crisscrossed the square, coats clutched close and heads bent against the wind. Jonah had a sudden longing to be out there, breathing real air, braced against the cold. Up here was all perfumed warmth and sleepy comfort. It was hard to think straight, as though he was walking in a dream that had broken into his waking life.

The lift to get here had been silent and fast. He'd never been in a lift and he wasn't keen on it. The building's quake-warning system was only as good as the glimpser on duty. What if they were sleeping, or high, and didn't raise the alarm? In a bad quake, wouldn't a lift just stop, mid-floor? Imagine being stuck for hours in that tiny space. He wondered about walking down the stairs at the end of this meeting.

The lift doors had opened on a wide sweep of grey carpet, subtle lighting, leather furniture, flowers in vases, water in carafes, and this astonishing view of the city. People glided quietly about, taking no notice of any of it.

The woman at the desk was talking to him and he turned to focus on what she was saying. She had to get what she called his 'backstory' for the show, but she seemed as happy to make it up as hear it from him. 'Ready?' she smiled. 'You're going to be famous, you know. People will want to know all about you. Let's start with your family.'

He explained the bare bones.

'Love it!' she said. 'Your father upped sticks and there's you left to care for your poor, invalid mother! The loyal son. This is great.'

'No! It's not like that. My dad keeps in touch. He sends money home.'

She gave a little shrug. 'Absent father, then. And how

is your mother? We'd like to get an interview with her.'

'She's…she's not recovered yet.'

'Oh. I see. A short piece to camera?'

He shook his head. 'She doesn't really talk at all.' He thought of how he'd seen her last night when he'd explained what he was about to do. He'd stood in the doorway of her room and watched her watch the moon rising through the tall east-facing window. She hadn't turned. He'd said, 'Hi, Mum,' and gone in, switching on the light. He'd kissed the top of her head and sat down beside her, putting her dinner on the side table, and she had turned her head and blinked at him. Slowly, lips and tongue working hard, she managed, 'Jonah.'

He'd smiled at her. 'That's my name. Don't wear it out.'

And so it had been for the months, now years, since the first quakes. Her improvement was there, notice-able but so very slow. And he'd wondered, as he always wondered, how she might have been if she'd had proper medical care. If he hadn't lost the money that would have paid for that. If he hadn't chased the illusion of PANN's promise.

The woman frowned and typed a note to herself. 'Right. Perhaps we could just have a picture of her? Or you could walk with her in a garden? Now, what about a girlfriend? Or boyfriend?'

And on it had gone, rolling through his life, smoothing

out its edges, bending it into a thumbnail account that he hardly recognised. There was a lot he didn't tell her, and some parts he made up, but on she went, filling in the gaps with her own imaginings.

One thing he didn't make up though, were his glimpses. 'We'll be recreating them,' she explained. 'And playing them on the show.' He told them to her true. For some reason he didn't understand, she'd stared at him after that and said, 'You really see all that?' He wished PANN could hear that he was giving GlimpseCorp what he'd never give to them. Also, he hoped whoever sent the glimpses would understand why he was doing this.

People at home thought the glimpses were warnings sent by the quake dead and that was a good enough explanation for him. It was important to keep faith with the quake dead and that was one reason he was nervous about all this—you mess with the glimpses, you disrespect the dead. And this felt like selling that gift. But he told himself that he wasn't really selling them. He was trading them to battle con artists and expose them and surely that would be okay.

When he came to his story about how PANN had conned him, the woman was avid for every detail. 'This is great…really great!' She paused then went on, 'But, of course, terrible. How terrible of them to trick you like that.'

'Will I be able to tell this on the show?'

'Of course. This will generate huge interest. I may have to run it by our lawyers. Do you have any evidence?'

'They admitted it! They said they'd moved her to a higher plane of existence. Do you think they won't stand by that?'

She studied him and made more notes then checked her watch. 'Now,' she said, 'I believe you're due to meet up with another guest for a night out?'

Her name was Audri and she was gorgeous. She was as tall as Jonah and she looked like she'd prepped for a winter holiday at someone's private lodge: she was snug in a long leather coat with a wide fur collar, her boots had needle-sharp heels, her long hair shone gold in the streetlights, her smile was red and curling in a let's-behave-badly kind of way, and she was very good at hiding her distaste at having to be out with this D-Zoner. Very good, but not perfect.

Audri seemed to think that his first language was Zone, a tongue unknown to modern urbanites, so she relieved him of the task of saying anything at all by talking non-stop. She was very excited about being a guest on the Glimpse Show. Her glimpse involved seeing a panther in a forest, which was awesome, wouldn't he agree? Everyone was talking about it. She'd already had some interest from would-be sponsors—fashion, hair and make-up people. Maybe even film producers.

Jonah was happy to let her talk. He had started to explain that he hadn't seen much of the show because the D-Zone didn't have reliable streaming, that it didn't even have reliable electricity, but she moved on to a detailed account of how she'd arranged for them to meet some friends for pizza and then go to a club—would that be all right, of course it would. Jonah wondered if she'd noticed that they were being followed.

The pizza bar was brimming with people and blasting with music; the air was a warm fug of perfumed bodies and the aroma of pizza and cocktails. Audri found her friends with a relief that was painfully obvious, and she introduced Jonah as though he was an exotic prize that she was baffled to have won. The friends were intrigued.

'Hey, are there pizzas in the D-Zone?'

'Sure.'

'Are they as good as this, though?'

'Um—'

'Cool tattoo. Does everyone have one?'

'A lot of people—'

'Why are you still living there?'

'I got friends there, family, you know.'

'Which gang are you in?'

'What?'

'What d'you think of the rebuild?'

'Round here? It's great. You'd hardly know there'd been any quakes—'

'Feel that quake last night?'

'Hard to miss.'

'Our glimpsers missed it. Didn't get any sirens or anything. My mum broke her ankle. We should sue them, that's what I reckon.'

Jonah glanced at Audri but she was occupied taking a selfie with a fan so he retreated to his pizza slice, which was, he had to admit, very good: crust super-thin and cheese super-stretchy—the sort of cheese that Art would actually cry over. The man who'd been following them was taking photos now. When Jonah pointed this out, Audri put down her pizza slice and sat up straighter. 'Oh, yes?' Her smile turned radiant as she looked around for her admirer. 'People recognise me all the time. I don't mind, you know.' But the man had vanished into the crowd and she seemed disappointed. The talk drifted off into chat about someone's job interview and someone else's problem finding an apartment, and some general moaning about the failed glimpse alarms, but Jonah had stopped paying attention because the big screen on the wall behind Audri was showing a sweeping drone shot of the D-Zone.

The drone was racing down streets towards the glow of the holo-shrine then it pulled up high into the sky so that the whole area was laid out below. There was no streetlighting and not even any building lights, which meant that the power was off—situation normal. But the holo-shrine shone like a jewel in the centre of that darkness, and bearing down on it, like threads in a shimmering spiderweb, lines of people were walking, holding small lights, torches, candle flames.

Someone was tapping his arm. 'You want more pizza?' It was an Audri hanger-on called Fitz. He was about Jonah's age and he had a haircut that Jonah thought could probably account for a month of Art and Nem's takings combined.

'No,' said Jonah. 'Thanks.' He turned back to the screen.

'Pretty crazy, what's going on there,' said Fitz. 'People coming here from all over for that anniversary. It's only a week or so away, right?'

Jonah nodded, eyes still on the screen.

'Hey, I know!' said Fitz. 'Let's check out our own Zoners. Whaddya say?'

'Your own Zoners?'

'Sure—Buskers' Alley. Heaps of Zoners end up there, trying to make a buck. I mean, they're mostly BTF, but y'know, some of them can do stuff. Tricks and that.'

'BTF?'

Fitz grinned. He had very straight, white teeth. 'Broke Travelling Folk.'

Jonah looked back at the screen so that he didn't break Fitz's pretty face.

'Great idea, babe,' said Audri. She dabbed at her

lips. 'I was planning on us going to the Windmill but that's way better.' She shot Jonah a mischievous smile. He considered escaping. He reckoned he could lose the tail without too much trouble. But he wanted to stay on the right side of GlimpseCorp; slipping his minders and losing his tail—he knew that they weren't going to love that. He gritted his teeth and prepared to be ashamed of his fellow D-Zoners begging on the roadside.

Buskers' Alley was no alley. It shifted nightly, sometimes morphing into multiple strands in different parts of the city, sometimes merging back into a single entity, a creature evolving to confound the police and the BCB who regularly broke up the Alley when they could find it. After all, they had targets to meet—tallies of illegals to arrest and ship off to Flint Point—and the Alley was a perfect hunting ground.

At times the police and the BCB fell over their own feet in their haste to get there first. Knowing that the two agencies were fierce rivals and would never trust each other's information, the buskers played them, planting clues of misdirection as to their whereabouts on any particular night. It worked pretty well. Some nights they were left completely alone.

Tonight, Buskers' Alley was in a grassy square and it wasn't at all what Jonah was expecting. It was bustling with acts and some of them were great. Streetlights shone yellow on the wet pavement around the square, while food trucks strung with coloured lights brightened the spaces in-between. They walked past a fire-breather, a silver-grey man still as a statue, crystal-ball gazers and palm readers, a small band of mime artists, and musicians of all ages and abilities playing everything from tin whistles to tubas.

Jonah wandered among them feeling strangely light and cheerful, as though everything he'd ever been anxious about had stayed back in the D-Zone and couldn't escape to plague him here. He had papers from Alphonsine in his pocket, paid for by GlimpseCorp itself, he had some spending money saved from his pizza work and he was on track, at last, to expose PANN for the fraudsters they really were.

He stopped to watch a juggler and thought about Bas. Bas would love it here—the old Bas, anyway, who would have run away and joined the circus if there had been a circus to join. Risk and reward, that was Bas. Had been Bas. Even if he was doing nothing more than trying to not drop a ball in an attempt at juggling, he always made it about life on the edge. Commit to a thing and then go for it. Sometimes without a whole lot of thought, but that was what Jonah was for. Had been for.

A screech of tyres startled Jonah. Black vans were sweeping in from both ends of the square, disgorging armed Border Control agents in riot gear. The buskers scattered with much yelling and pushing. Fear of the BCB is second nature to D-Zoners and Jonah started to run. Then he remembered that, for once, he was legit. He stood his ground and looked around for Audri and Fitz. Papers were one thing, but being in fancy company probably offered more protection.

The agents were busy rounding up the buskers and it looked as though Audri and her friends were going to get away without a second look. And sure enough, an agent took one look at her and smiled, then at Fitz and smiled again. One up for the expensive haircut, thought Jonah. Then the guy looked at Jonah and said to Audri, 'Do you know this person?'

'Er,' she said. And that was all it took.

The agent pushed Jonah backwards away from Audri and Fitz. 'Gimme your papers. Do it slow.'

Heart thumping, Jonah took his ID out of his pocket slowly, with one hand, the way you did in the D-Zone.

The guy peered from the ID to Jonah and back again, frowning. Audri and Fitz watched, unspeaking. Jonah went cold with anger.

'Temporary papers?' said the agent.

'Sure,' said Jonah. 'Just waiting for the final word to come through.' He looked straight at Audri and smiled as he said, 'I'm going on the Glimpse Show. We're together.'

The agent looked at Audri. She blushed, whether from shame at disowning Jonah a moment ago or from embarrassment that he was claiming a connection with her, Jonah couldn't tell and didn't care. It was a sweet blush that the agent couldn't resist. His expression softened. He scrawled an authorisation on Jonah's ID and handed it back, saying, 'You young folk best get out of here tonight.'

One up for Alphonsine, thought Jonah. He turned away from the agent and that's when the glimpse hit.

It charged up his body from the ground and nearly knocked him flat. He crouched down, steadying himself with a palm on the ground while it raced through him and when it was gone and had left only its echo of nausea and fear, he got to his feet, hands on knees until the dizziness left him, then he did what he always did: stood up, put his hands to his mouth and yelled, 'QUAAAAKE!'

The arrests in progress nearby came to a halt as agents and buskers looked at him uncertainly. Some buskers took their chance and ran.

Audri gave him a horrified stare and hissed, 'What are you doing? The warning system hasn't been triggered.' She turned to Fitz, whispered loudly, 'A bit of attention-seeking from our newbie,' and stalked off.

Seconds later the earth roared like a freight train, the ground pitched, trees shook, streetlights died. People shouted and swore and clung to each other. Jonah rode it out, cold with fear for Evie and everyone at the Matterhorn.

When the earth settled at last, sirens and alarms were blasting across the city and people were flooding onto the streets from nearby buildings. Someone shouted for a medic, someone else slapped Jonah on the back and murmured, 'Thanks, kid.'

Jonah got out his phone and tried to call Evie. No luck, of course. After a quake this big, there would be plenty of aftershocks, people would charge about, checking on friends and family. There would be a rush on food and fuel. There would be traffic and crowds.

Audri and Fitz straightened up and Audri lifted her chin in defiance at him as if to say, 'Don't think this makes you any better than you are.'

Jonah turned away without a word and set out for home thinking about whether he'd rather do battle with the BCB or the shaking earth. They both sent his blood pounding and his heart racing. They both inspired deep fear among everyone in the D-Zone. The difference was, the earth wasn't out to get you, it didn't hate you, it didn't want you dead. It was just doing what it did and if you got in the way, well, that was shit bad luck. The BCB, though, that was a gun pointed, literally, in your face, daring you to resist and hoping that you would.

13

'OUR D-ZONE BOY,' said Kerryn Duval to Morgan.

'He'll do,' said Morgan. 'Not exactly star material, bit too shy for that, but he'll do.' He perched on the side of her desk and watched her multitask. 'He glimpsed the quake last night.' She looked up at him and he went on, 'I haven't told him he's the only one around here that did. Princess Audri didn't glimpse a damn thing, by the way. She says she did but our man was filming them and she clearly didn't have a clue. She's a fraud.'

'A glamorous fraud, though.'

'She threatens the credibility of the Show.'

Duval laughed out loud. 'She what? Nonsense. We do have a problem however, and it isn't her.'

'I know.' Morgan stood up and walked over to the window, looking out at the chaos still clogging the streets after last night's quake. Large flakes of snow were starting to fall. 'The Fade is happening faster than we expected. We are going to run out of recruits soon.'

'That's true.' She hesitated. 'Or rather, partially true. According to Dr What's-his-name they're still glimpsing in the D-Zone. He has a theory.'

He turned back to her. 'Dr Fisher. What's his theory?'

'Something to do with it being a gangland nirvana populated by illegals without any rebuild in prospect, so everyone lives on the edge of their nerves and that makes them hypersensitive to coming quakes. Sound plausible? I've no idea. But it's useful to us that that place is still a hotbed of glimpsers. But that's not the problem either.'

'Okay. What is the problem?'

She pushed her glossy bob behind one ear and studied a desktop screen. 'This boy.' She looked up at him. 'Have you seen the anniversary episode run sheet?'

'Of course. We had to rush it through, but it's good. He's our main guest. Standard start—he has a seriously detailed glimpse, by the way. Then Zac gets going with childhood stuff—also pretty good. Tough life. And for the grand finale, we have the People for a New Nation exposed as frauds, literally taking money from a child. Shock, horror, scandal. It'll be great for ratings. Just what we need. We'll have all the usual disclaimers, of course. We could even go and talk to this PANN brother and sister if you like.'

'Replace him.'

'What?'

'Replace him with another guest or pull the special entirely.'

'You're not serious.'

'I am deadly serious.'

'But—'

'You're not listening. Do it.'

'Our most gripping episode ever? That we've already trailed widely. I have to ask why.'

'You can ask all you like.' She turned back to her screen.

'All right, I'm asking.'

'Lawyers,' she said shortly. 'Our lawyers won't let us traduce PANN.'

'Bullshit, if you'll pardon my language. We have any number of ways of doing it without liability. We *need* this, Kerryn. We need it to survive.'

She sighed and pushed back her chair.

'You'd better tell me what's going on,' he said.

She stood up, folding her arms and joined him at the window. 'Phaedra is not returning my calls.'

'Phaedra? The sister?'

'Yes of course the sister.'

'What do you mean she's not returning your calls? Why are you calling her? How do you even know her?'

'We have an agreement. PANN is supposed to be attracting glimpsers in the D-Zone and funnelling them to us. At first the idea was to give us an ongoing supply for the Glimpse Show. But once the city's quake-warning system started failing for want of glimpsers, I saw an opportunity. If we can get access to enough glimpsers we can run the warning system. It will suit the city because most of those glimpsers are illegals, so the city can't employ them. But if the city pays us and we pay the glimpsers, then those problems can slide, no questions asked. It would be a nice little earner for us, but more importantly'—she turned to him—'we are Glimpse Corporation. We're not just about light entertainment. We're pitching to City Hall here, and to City Halls everywhere, to be the company that runs glimpse quake-warning systems. Do you see how big this could be? Every city has their D-Zone—there will always be places where things are too broken to fix and people are living on the very edge. That's where we'll find our glimpsers.'

'Wait, wait, wait,' Morgan held up both hands. 'You're losing me. We've had someone in the D-Zone for months trying to recruit glimpsers for the Show and they've managed to recruit precisely one. And you want to cut him loose.'

'Precisely one, as you say, because PANN hasn't been playing ball, despite our agreement. They've kept the glimpsers they've found and generated their own quite ludicrous narrative about all this. But I still have hopes of getting them back on board, and that won't happen if we do a show-and-tell on their donations practices.' She paused and studied the snow swirling into the square below.

'Look, illegals aren't going to come straight to a big shiny corporation to proclaim their glimpsing abilities; that's far too risky. They need to know we can be trusted first, and PANN was supposed to do that work for us. Earn their trust, and feed them through. That was the deal. I don't know why they've gone rogue on me. Perhaps they've started believing their own claptrap. They've got people in the D-Zone treating the glimpses as visions of their so-called New Nation rising up from the ashes of the old world. I intend to remind them that they have a job to do, for which they've been richly rewarded.'

They stared out at the snow. Then Morgan said, 'How richly?'

She frowned. 'Richly enough that I'd like some return on this rather urgently.'

'Before the Board sees the books?'

'If you like.'

'I see. Call the other sibling, then. The brother.'

She snorted. 'Damon wouldn't answer a call from me if the world really was ending.' She walked away, back to her desk. 'Cut the boy loose.'

'What about the advance we gave him?'

'Get it back, obviously. Now go and do your work and stop bothering me.'

14

SHIKHA STARED AT the 'Expect Delays' sign plastered across the platform noticeboard at the station and longed for a cab. After her meeting with the dead-eyed Mr Morgan this morning, she knew that she might never be able to afford a cab again. And she could kiss her dreams of directing episodes of the Glimpse Show good-bye. Also, her career progression in GlimpseCorp was a goner. And the sting in the tale? Morgan had informed her that it was her job to tell Jonah the bad news. She had gaped at him, but he hadn't even had the decency to look embarrassed. Or bothered to say thank you, or goodbye. He'd ushered her briskly out of his office with the air of someone who had urgent business and closed the door on her.

She joined the small crowd that had huddled under the platform's meagre shelter watching the rain drip and puddle and looking forlornly along the track. There was a nanosecond of excitement when a man in a hi-vis vest nudged through them and peeled off the delay sign, but he replaced it with an All-Trains-Cancelled sign and the hope dispersed like air from a popped balloon. Last night's quake had not been kind to train tracks.

Shikha had to ask Jonah to pay the money back, but she was certain that he had even less money than she did. Morgan had told her if she couldn't pay the lump sum back immediately, they would deduct it from her wages. It would take months.

Those people that always took delays and cancellations as a personal affront were swearing and waving their hands about, then they marched off to find someone to complain to, but there was no one in the ticket office to take complaints because there was no longer a ticket office: the people running the trains knew a thing or two. Shikha turned for home.

What was she supposed to tell Jonah? Sorry, we've canned your episode where you were finally going to see some small measure of justice for your family by exposing a corrupt cult. It's just a pity that it didn't fit the schedule any more.

The downpour was drenching now, thudding the street so hard that foot sloggers were saturated from above and below. The signs on buildings were bleary through the pelting rain and what street lamps there were had come on far too early, as though the man in charge of them had been feeling munificent, or perhaps he'd decided that the lure of beer and a burger beat hanging around the office in weather like this, so he'd thrown the switch and gone home. It took only a few minutes for Shikha to be thoroughly soaked.

She should, she knew, have been heading for her stall in the D-Zone. But for what? To spend another fruit-less night freezing her backside off in the service of a company that didn't care one jot about its employees or, as it turned out, any glimpsers she might find.

She hardly saw the people she was splashing and bumping into, although she did get an inkling that her current knowledge of terms of abuse on the street was woefully inadequate. When she got to her doorstep, she stepped inside and looked at her dismal little rented room: it was cold, it was beige, it smelled of the damp and, worst of all, it was empty. Dinner was sitting in packets in the cupboard. If there was to be a welcome home cup of hot chocolate, or bowl of soup, or glass of wine, she would be serving it to herself.

An image crossed her mind then, of the warm kitchen at the Matterhorn, the fire blazing, dinner simmering on the stove, the place abuzz with people interested in each other's lives. Yes, it was also incredibly dangerous. Nobody was ever going to lob a home-made explosive into her beige bedsit, but no one was going to celebrate it either, certainly not her. She stood there for a moment longer, then she turned back into the rain, locking the door behind her.

15

JONAH LEANED AGAINST a back corner of the church, closed his eyes and listened to the chat around him. The music had been turned down some, now that everyone was gathered inside and the PANN siblings were about to arrive. Five days to go. Five days and then it was all on. The atmosphere in the church was breathless, devout, drunk even, with the promise of what was to come.

Jonah looked for Bas and saw him up near the front, hair cut pilgrim short, wearing one of those stupid blue tunics. He was surrounded, crowded, by other pilgrims. Every now and then the man next to him bent close and murmured something, or touched him on the shoulder to get his attention, or exchanged a smile like a secret shared.

Bas was in deep now. The bluster that his mother used to call his bull charm had gone. Back when the quakes began, Bas used to just do stuff that needed doing without asking or checking that he was following the rules. His mother told him off in public for his cheek, but when no one was looking she was proud as any mother could be whose kid is turning out great. Bas and his giant-sized grin lunged at everything and Jonah was always running to keep up. But that was a long time ago. These days Bas was full of B-S and couldn't see a pack of lies when it was staring him in the face.

A sudden blast of music had all heads turning to the doors as Phaedra and Damon walked in, arm in arm, and glided up the centre aisle. Hands reached out to touch them and people called their names. The place was packed, people lining the walls and squeezing shoulder to shoulder into the space where the seats used to be. Outsiders were arriving every day now and Jonah reckoned that the crowd tonight was about half and half local and out-of-towner.

Phaedra and Damon reached the front, silence fell, and Phaedra launched into her Words of Wisdom for the week. 'We're here tonight, my friends, for one special reason.' Her voice was clear, lilting, easy as the music that murmured beneath it. 'And what is that reason?' She smiled into the hopeful silence then raised her arms. 'Because we know what's coming!'

A cheer went up. Jonah dug his hands in his pockets thinking that no, no one knew what was coming because the siblings weren't telling. They were just hinting at vague promises and leaving their followers to fill in the blanks.

'A great transformation is coming!' cried Phaedra. 'One that will change your lives forever!'

'YES!' shouted the crowd.

Phaedra nodded her approval and they basked in that glow. 'Do you feel like you've been ignored, my friends? Do you feel that you've been left in the rubble by City Hall? Left to rot? Is that how it feels?'

Yelling and stamping of feet.

'Well, I'm here to tell you. You haven't been ignored— oh no. Did you know?' Her eyes swept the crowd. 'That you are being watched? Oh, yes. Spies are here among us.'

Jonah held still, not meeting any gaze that might come his way. Evie had wanted to come tonight. Jonah had argued that because he was Bas's friend, or had been, he could be considered a possible convert, something no one would believe of Evie. She had met this with a reluctant shrug and, to his relief, had agreed to stay away.

'And why?' Phaedra was almost whispering. People leaned in. 'Friends, make no mistake. Spies are here, watching you and reporting back to City Hall, because City Hall is afraid.'

Her voice soared again. 'Of YOU! They are afraid of you. Soon you will see a build-up of police and troops around here. Oh, yes. Because it's coming. In just five days! A great moment of liberation! And I have one question for you. ARE YOU READY?'

The cheering all but raised the roof.

Jonah watched, unmoved.

'So!' Phaedra smiled and opened her arms to embrace her audience. 'They have a problem, over there at City Hall. And what is that problem? It's us! They weren't expecting that you would learn the truth! That in just five days, one great quake, the last quake, will usher in a great transformation. And together we will step free into a new world. A world that many of you have already glimpsed. There will be no restrictions or laws but those we make ourselves. No one will have power over us. You'll run your own lives, the way you want! And there will be abundance! Just as the earth has destroyed so much, the earth will provide even more.'

Her voice softened into longing. 'And you are the bringers of this transformation. Did you think your glimpsing was for nothing? By no means! You who are so close to the Earth that she speaks to you and through you will be rewarded by her with generous bounty.'

There was cheering and whooping and music swelling as she went on.

'And the people out there in the plaza—the ones we loved and still love? Soon, my friends, soon, your grief for them will turn to joy.'

This was the lie that held Bas captive. This hint, and it was only ever spoken as a hint, that in the energy released by a supposedly great quake, the holos would step from the panels that generated them and walk back into life.

Jonah would smash this lie if he knew how. He looked at Bas's upturned face, at all the upturned faces here, and had a powerful urge to kick a rats' nest—any rats' nest would do as long as it erupted in a swarm of spitting, fighting vermin that *woke people up*. That woke Bas up, especially. Jonah wanted mayhem and chaos and fight. The world had got buttoned down and hushed and everyone was holding their breath for something that would never happen. These people weren't worrying about the BCB coming back, or the daily power cuts, or that food was hard to get, or that their phone and web connectivity was almost non-existent. They thought that PANN was protecting them, and that their lives were divided into Before and Now: before PANN, before the holo shrine, back in the old days, as if those days were on the edge of living memory instead of just a few weeks ago.

Now the collection bags were coming around and Damon was stepping forward, raking the crowd with those clouded eyes, as though he could see everyone, see through them. 'Will you be ready?' he called. 'I can see— oh, yes, folks—I can see what you cannot.' He swept the air with his hands. 'I see goodness out there!'

'Yes!' cried the crowd.

'And I see sorrow!'

'Yes!'

'And I see struggle!'

'Yes! Yes!'

'And I see hope! That's what I see. I see hope! It's coming, people! It's coming here! And we'll be ready. Anybody out there not going to be ready?'

'No, sir!'

'And who out there glimpsed last week? Come forward! We need your help to build the pathway to a new world! Come on, now! Don't be shy.'

People stood up or raised their hands. Jonah thought of Shikha in her market stall, sitting lonely all these past months, waiting for these very people. No wonder she hadn't found them.

There were plenty coming forward. They would talk into the night now, relating the glimpses that came with last week's quakes. And Damon would nod as he listened, as though there was some secret encoded into the glimpses that only he could read.

Jonah had had his own glimpses, of course, but that wasn't their business. Jonah's glimpses were between him and this unsteady land he was standing on.

These past few weeks, the splinters of sky in his glimpse had been winter grey, the trees were bare of leaves and the air was a cold blast. His glimpses still filled him with dread and awe; it was like the planet was breaking into his mind, haunting him, reminding him how old it was, and how temporary he was.

He sought out Bas again and watched him for a few more minutes, then turned and slipped through the crowd by the door and out onto the steps where the dark was cold and blustery and the plaza was empty except for the smiling, shining dead.

Evie was still up when Jonah got home. He kissed her and asked how her dad was. 'Cheerful,' said Evie. 'I don't know where he gets that from. Maybe it's the painkillers. He has no right to be cheerful! He's going to come out of this half blind but he's lying there holding my hand and smiling at me and telling me things will be fine. He's just a very sweet man.'

They went into the kitchen while Jonah ate a slab of cheese-and-spinach pie left over from dinner and Evie made hot chocolate for her uncle, Raynor, who was upstairs on the graveyard shift for Matterhorn watch.

'Oh, by the way,' said Evie, 'Shikha's here. She's sleeping in the sunroom.'

'Okay,' said Jonah. 'Why is she here?'

'She wants to talk to you. Something about the Glimpse Show, I guess. Came all the way on her own, which is brave. How was the rally? Tell me everything.'

'It was crazy. They're talking about spies now. For

City Hall. They're everywhere apparently. Non-existent spies and fairy-tale promises, that about sums it up.'

'And Bas?'

'Right up the front like he belongs. He's wearing the blue tunic now.'

'He'll come back, you'll see.'

Jonah finished his pie and went to wash his dishes. 'He won't. Not while they're here.'

The day before, Jonah had been doing pizza prep ahead of the market and he'd heard someone call his name. Several someones. He'd made his way through the onlookers crowding the holo memorial towards the commotion.

At the heart of the uproar was Bas, waving an empty bottle at people who were pressing round. He tried to lean on the holo of Stanley Fielding, who used to run a bakery on Parkview Rd. But this Stanley Fielding was made of light and nothing else, and Bas kept falling over.

One of his pilgrim buddies was there—Jonah couldn't remember his name—trying to grab him and move him away. The crowd was muttering about people disrespecting their dead and the PANN guy kept looking around as though the reinforcements he'd ordered were taking their sweet time.

Bas spied Jonah and came up to wave the bottle in his face, staring at him with wide, wild eyes. 'Hey!' His breath was so ripe it'd be risky to strike a match.

'Hey.' Jonah swayed to avoid the bottle. 'What are you doing?'

'My mum and Lily—they're gone! I looked! I looked everywhere!' He swung an arm wide, the bottle flew loose, everybody ducked, and it smashed on the ground four holos over. Bas watched wide-eyed then swung round to stare at Jonah. 'Didn't mean to do that, okay?' Then he swayed and muttered, 'Feel sick.' He doubled over and emptied his stomach next to Jonah's boots.

'Thanks,' said Jonah. 'C'mon. Let's go home.'

Bas grabbed both of Jonah's arms. 'But where are they?' He was close to tears, his face taut. 'I can't...I can't find them.'

'Jeez, Bas.' Jonah put an arm round his shoulders. 'Come home, okay?'

Then the reinforcements arrived: two blue-tunic guys, both older, and burly with it. They ignored Jonah. 'Sebastian!' said one of them. 'Come with us and we'll make sure your mother and sister are restored.'

'Hold up!' Jonah's arm tightened around Bas. 'He doesn't need you looking after him. He's got friends who can do that. C'mon Bas.' He started to guide Bas away.

But Bas stopped, frowning. 'Wait...just wait a sec.' He turned to the pilgrims. 'Where are they?'

'They'll be restored soon. If you come with us now.' The guy stood still and tall, sinister with calm.

Bas fixed him with an almost-steady stare. 'Promise?'

'No!' said Jonah. 'They're lying! They always lie! It's what they do.'

'Of course, I promise,' said the pilgrim. 'Come with me. Now.'

Bas turned to Jonah. 'I'll just…I'll just go,' he slurred. 'So's I can find them again. Okay? I have to. I have to, cos when the big quake comes…'

Jonah was pleading now. 'They're not real, Bas! It's not them! They died and they're not coming back. They're not! Look!' He swept a hand through Stanley Fielding. 'It's nothing. It's light and air. That's all.' He walked right through Stanley, then back to stand in front of Bas. 'See?' People gasped and called out and one of the pilgrims grabbed Jonah's arm and pulled him away from the holo. Jonah swung a fist but only connected with air.

Bas watched, blinking, then stepped up to Jonah. 'You don't do that,' he slurred. He pushed Jonah back two steps. 'You don't do that. Ever.' He pushed him again. The pilgrim buddies were closing in, grabbing him.

Jonah pushed them off. 'He doesn't need you!' he yelled. One of the pilgrims put an arm around Bas's shoulders and steered him away. 'He doesn't need you!' Jonah yelled again. But Bas was gone and the crowd broke up, giving Jonah filthy looks and a wide berth.

Then this morning, soul-sick and angry, Jonah was prowling around the Matterhorn not knowing what to do with himself, when Bas arrived.

'Hey.' Jonah's heart lifted with surprise and relief.

'Oh,' said Bas. 'Hey. Just here to collect my stuff.'

Jonah's relief drained away. He followed Bas to the room they shared and Bas started throwing things into a backpack.

'What happened to your face?' Jonah asked.

Bas's cheekbone was red and puffy, almost burnt-looking. 'I'm coming clean.'

'You're what?'

Bas pulled the cord tight on the top of his backpack and stood up. 'That ink?' he pointed at the faultline tattoo on Jonah's face. 'It's a tie to this world, the old order. I'm ditching it.'

'The old order? Bas—'

'Don't need it. Not with what's coming.' He hefted the bag onto his shoulder, looked around the room and gave a sharp nod. Then his gaze came back to Jonah. 'Come with me. I don't want to leave you behind.'

'Are they back? Your holos?'

'Yeah.'

'Bas! It's how they control people. Anytime anyone does something they don't like, down go their holos. And they don't go back up until people fall into line.'

Bas shook his head. The scar on his face was red and angry but his eyes were bright. 'I'm not gonna be part of the old order anymore. You shouldn't either. Come and find me when you come to your senses. I'll be waiting.'

He walked past Jonah, down the hall and away.

'Bas!'

'Don't leave it too long!' Bas called back and kept on walking.

Pondering on this, Jonah finished washing his plate, but he stayed with his back to Evie, wiping the sink with a dishcloth till long after it was clean. She came over and peered at his face. 'Hey.' She put a hand on his back.

He shook his head, then turned around and put his arms around her. 'I wouldn't have picked it. Him going off like that. Walking away. Following them. I mean Bas isn't a follower.' He gave a short laugh. 'That's me, I'm the follower. But there he goes. Giving up all this to go after those clowns.'

She pulled back and looked up at him. 'Giving up you?'

He was silent then and she stood on tiptoe and kissed his cheek.

'I guess,' he said.

He kissed her forehead and gave himself a mental shake. 'What will happen when nothing happens? That's what I want to know. They're not talking about putting the world back together bit by bit, the way we've all been doing for years. They talk like they're gonna replace it all in an instant; suddenly your worries will be over and your dead will come walking back to you. I mean, it's a grief dream, I get that. But when it doesn't happen, what then? Who gets the blame?'

Evie smiled. 'We do, obviously. The unbelievers.'

'And why doesn't that scare you?' He gave her an affectionate shake. 'It scares the hell out of me.'

'It does scare me. Believe me it does. But they're not going to drive us out. And once you go on that show and tell the world about PANN, just you wait and see how many other people come forward with the same story. It'll be the beginning of an avalanche. The beginning of the end. And then, I'm sure, Bas will come back. What? You don't believe me?'

'I want to.'

She grinned. 'So, do.'

And he thought, but did not say: What if I lose you too?

16

IN THE SUNROOM of the Matterhorn, Shikha slept long and deep, feeling unaccountably safe. She woke to sunlight through the window and a fresh sprinkling of snow on the garden and orchard. A few minutes later she was sitting at the kitchen table with Evie and Jonah, drinking coffee and eating toast and delivering bad news.

The bad news had Jonah getting up from the table and walking away to stare out a window. He stood looking at the garden for a while, then came back, sat down next to Evie and swore.

Evie took his hand. 'I'm so sorry. What are you going to do now?'

Jonah picked her hand up and kissed it. 'You mean am I going to do something stupid? Asks the person who won't move out of her house even though it's been fire-bombed and she's on a WANTED list.'

'No, that's not what I mean. Well,' Evie smiled, 'not entirely.'

'A what list?' said Shikha.

'They've got this list,' said Jonah. 'Of so-called deceivers. Everyone in the choir is on it.'

'Weird,' said Shikha. 'What does it mean?'

Evie shrugged. 'Anyone who's spoken out against them is on that list.'

'And what happens to people on the list?'

'They haven't said.' Jonah poured more coffee. 'So far, they've told their followers to not believe anything the deceivers say. But they're gonna blame the people on that list when their precious new world doesn't arrive next week.'

Shikha looked at Evie. 'They've painted a target on your back.'

Evie nodded. 'Seems so.'

'Which is why,' said Jonah, 'you should get out of here. Just for the week. Just till it's all calmed down again.'

This was clearly a conversation that was both ongoing and, as far as Shikha could tell, fruitless. Jonah opened his arms wide and high, 'Aaaargh!' then collapsed back to the table. 'It was gonna be so sweet. Huge audience. Moment of truth. All kinds of drama. Those bastards. You don't know why they ditched me?'

Shikha shook her head. 'No idea, I'm sorry.'

'Well,' said Jonah. 'I'm not gonna let it lie. Not now that they've got Bas.'

'They've got Bas?' said Shikha. 'Oh, no.'

Jonah nodded. 'Yeah, well, I'm still going to find a way to tell the world what they are. It's not like everyone has turned pilgrim; the ones who have are really loud, so it looks like there's loads of them but a lot of those are visitors who won't hang around when it all goes pear-shaped. Heaps of other people have doubts and I want them to know that they're right.'

'The loud ones are dangerous though,' said Shikha. 'How's your dad?' she asked Evie.

'Not good,' said Evie. 'He's lost an eye and he has a head injury—we don't know how that will go yet. His other injuries are healing okay.'

'And your mother?'

'Rattled,' said Evie. 'She wouldn't want anyone to know that, of course. She just carries on looking out for people regardless of any threat to her.'

'Sound familiar?' muttered Jonah.

'She spends most of her time helping at the clinic,' said Evie. 'And Mikey's staying with friends.'

'Have there been more attacks?' asked Shikha.

'Not here. But we can't get into the church now; they've set guards on the door and only pilgrims are allowed in. They tried to do that with access to the holos too, but people weren't having it. There were some nasty moments and some people got hurt. Phaedra's all, *we're about peace and love*, but that's obviously B-S. But we're careful around here. There's a roster—you might have noticed. Someone's on watch 24/7.'

'You do realise,' said Shikha to Jonah, 'that if you had told your story on the Glimpse Show these lunatics would have turned their guns—maybe literally—on you?'

'I'd be in good company.'

'You need more people. Not just you two.'

'We're working on it,' said Evie.

Then Jonah asked the question Shikha was hoping for and dreading. 'Do GlimpseCorp want their money back?'

She grimaced. 'Yeah. They do.'

He narrowed his eyes at her. 'Were you going to tell me?'

'Um. Sure.'

'I will pay it back.'

'What if he didn't?' said Evie to Shikha. 'What would happen?'

Shikha gazed down at the table top. 'Comes out of my wages.'

'Ouch,' said Evie.

Shikha said, 'I don't suppose that lady…'

'Alphonsine?' said Jonah.

'Yes, her. I don't suppose she'd give us a break? A loan?'

'Getting in debt to people here, it's not a great idea,' said Jonah. 'I'll pay you back. It might take a while.'

'We should ask her,' said Evie.

Jonah's eyebrows shot up.

'What?' said Evie. 'She might give us a loan. Her terms would be better than anyone's. It's not right that Shikha gets punished for this.'

A few hours later the three of them were sipping tea with Alphonsine—a warming chai this time, spiced with orange peel, cinnamon and cloves. Outside, the wind was whining and snow was tumbling through the empty skylights. But inside Alphonsine's apartment there was warmth and colour and gentle candlelight.

The high ceilings, tall windows and polished wooden floors were beautiful in a shabby kind of way. Shikha wondered how she kept the place warm, especially when there was snow settling on the stairs and balconies right outside her door. She must be rich, Shikha decided, and wondered how rich. A pile of cash squirrelled away in a spare pillowcase in the linen closet? No, she thought. The more she watched the mystery and strange beauty of this woman the more she thought that a spare pillowcase wouldn't do it: somewhere out there, in the basement of a bank so secret that almost no one had heard of it, Alphonsine surely had a fortune lying at ease in a strongbox.

Alphonsine watched Evie explain about needing a loan, then she shook her head and said to Jonah, 'You're a bad risk. You make yourself a target, then you get hurt or killed, then I won't get my money back. How much longer do you have with those papers? A few weeks? For your own good, I should take them back and repay you half the fee. This is unheard of, I know, but I am willing to offer that.'

Jonah opened his mouth but Alphonsine held up a hand, forestalling his protest. 'I know. You are committed. That being so, I have news for you. Which I shouldn't be telling you because it will spur you on. However.' She poured more tea into each of their cups and handed round the plate of chocolate truffles that they had all been eyeing but were too polite to dive on.

She sat back, dusting imaginary crumbs from her lap. 'GlimpseCorp is coming to the D-Zone. They plan a live stream of the events of the seventh anniversary in a few days' time. If you survive that, you shall have your loan.'

'A live stream!' said Jonah and Shikha together.

'Brilliant!' said Jonah. He turned to Shikha. 'Do you know any of the crew? Could you get me in with one of them?'

'No,' said Shikha. 'I don't. Because I work in the basement and nobody knows I exist. Dammit. I can't believe this. They're going to do an anniversary special after all. That was my idea!'

'Also—' Alphonsine cast a quelling look at Shikha— 'something has happened of more importance than this.' When she had their attention, she said, 'You may know that when the Downtown East area was declared a demolition zone, City Hall bought the land; they paid out the owners of the buildings and land here that were declared unrecoverable—paltry sums, but still. Those who could, took their money and left. Undocumented individuals could not, of course, make any claim on this money. Well, now we come to it. GlimpseCorp has bought the D-Zone from City Hall. For a negligible sum, I believe.'

'Whaaat?' said Evie. 'Why?'

'That I do not know,' said Alphonsine. 'Perhaps they mean to develop it, but the land is so rotten that it will cost a gargantuan sum to rehabilitate. Not to mention the cost of demolishing what is currently broken here.'

Shikha was frowning. 'Why would they do this? It's not like they've got real-estate ambitions. Or not that I know of. Do you think they'll sell it on?'

'Who would buy?' said Alphonsine. 'That is all I have for you. May I suggest that, for the next few days at least, you do not underestimate the bigotry of zealots.'

Shikha went home, she went to work, she watched the news. The headlines continued to fret about the failure of the city's glimpse-warning system, but no one official was prepared to say why it had failed. The message from on high was clear: no need to panic, there would be a review, everything was in hand.

Meanwhile, thousands of people were flooding into the D-Zone for the anniversary. Some were arriving on foot, waving banners, some chugged up in overcrowded elderly house buses, some formed chanting processions and a few had turned up as austere singles. Hopes were high. Money, Shikha had no doubt, was flowing freely into PANN's collection bags.

She looked in vain for any news about Glimpse-Corp's deal to purchase the D-Zone. She watched news programs, social media feeds from the mainstream out to the wildest fringes, she even bought a newspaper. Nothing. Either it hadn't happened, or GlimpseCorp's higher-ups had reason for secrecy. She wondered how reliable Alphonsine was. This could just be rumour and hearsay gleaned from Alphonsine's ear to the ground. But even if that's all it was, she suspected that that ear, with its beautifully turned gemstone earring, heard things that normal people could not.

What she kept coming back to was this: Morgan had stolen her idea. Of course he had. How naïve she'd been, slogging away in the D-Zone, doing her job, finding a glimpser at last, then just handing him over to Morgan. Along with—she was furious she'd done this—a great idea for an anniversary special! And Morgan had marched away with it, while nixing the most important part, which was Jonah getting his chance at justice.

No doubt Morgan was, right now, getting kudos for his initiative. Maybe even a pay rise. And here she was, back in the basement, bored to death by gulls who thought they were glimpsing but were mainly jumping at their own shadows.

She wanted out. Out of the basement, certainly. Out of this job, maybe. But before she abandoned ship altogether, there was one tactic she thought she could try, if she was brave enough.

At midday, Shikha waited for Kerryn Duval's haughty PA to take her lunchbreak. She'd never met the PA let alone the CEO, but she had decided to go straight to the top. She was done with subtlety now; it was time to show ambition and initiative. She had one chance at this and if she only reached out as far as Morgan that chance would go nowhere.

She followed the PA down the steps and across the square to a cafe where a smiling waiter ushered the woman to a crisply-linened table in the window. Shikha found her way blocked by the same waiter who looked at her as though she was genuinely and tragically lost. Shikha patted down her unruly hair, smiled shyly to indicate that eating here was indeed well beyond her wildest dreams and said, 'I beg your pardon. I have an urgent message from Ms Duval for Ms Harran.' The man glanced fondly in the direction of Ms Harran and whispered, 'One moment.' He stalked away to the table by the window.

More whispering and some discreet pointing followed. The woman frowned and gave a tiny elegant shrug and Shikha was ushered to her table, the waiter shadowing her every step.

The PA dismissed him and raised her perfect eyebrows at Shikha. 'I don't know you. Who are you?'

'I'm from the basement. I want to see Ms Duval,' said Shikha.

The woman smiled faintly and sipped her water. 'Make an appointment.'

'That's not going to cut it, though, is it. She's always going to be too busy to see me.'

'Then I can't help you. Perhaps you should return to the basement and write a request.' She raised the eyebrows again and lifted a manicured finger towards the waiter.

'It's about a recent transaction between GlimpseCorp and City Hall relating to the D-Zone.' The PA frowned and the waiter was waved away. Then she leaned forward and all but hissed, 'What do you think you're doing?'

Shikha leaned in herself and smiled sweetly. 'Making an appointment.'

Which is how she came to be summoned back to the

thirty-ninth floor. But it wasn't Kerryn Duval she was seeing. It was the dreadful Morgan.

He closed the door of the small, windowless interview room where she'd been put and leaned back on it. 'I don't understand,' he said conversationally. 'Why are you here?'

Shikha stood up so that the man didn't tower over her. 'I'm requesting a position on the anniversary special.' She wondered if she should add, *since it was my idea*, but left that for later should it be needed.

'I see.' He turned away, sat down in one of the chairs, crossed his legs and leaned back to look at her. 'And you think you have some leverage.'

Now, standing up felt like being a school kid in front of the principal, waiting for a telling off. Shikha realised she had a few things to learn about power plays. She gave a little shrug, aiming for nonchalance, and sat down herself. 'I think there are a lot of people who would like to know about the deal GlimpseCorp has made to buy the D-Zone. Not least, D-Zone people themselves.'

He inspected his fingernails. 'And where did you hear this rumour? Because that's all it is.'

'Obviously, I'm not going to tell you. But it's from a cast-iron source.' Confidence was everything at this point.

There was an agonising pause. Then Morgan said, 'And what did you say you wanted?'

'A role in the anniversary special. I don't know if

you remember, but I suggested the idea to you and I'm excited that it's been picked up.' This was as near to a dig at him as she was going to permit herself.

Another pause. He narrowed his eyes at her, then gave a shrug. 'You'd have to sign an agreement, including a non-disclosure clause. Then possibly you could carry some bags.' He stood up. 'I'm in no way acknowledging the truth of anything you claim, by the way. I hope that's clear. But I'm always happy to help someone who's starting out on their career.'

17

'WE'RE TAKING THE church back,' said Evie.

'Okay,' said Jonah. 'Good. How exactly?'

They were lying on beanbags in front of the fire; everyone else, apart from the look-out upstairs, had gone to bed.

'We'll wait for the GlimpseCorp cameras to arrive,' said Evie. 'Shikha says they're coming tomorrow afternoon and they plan to stay until the clocks tick over to the anniversary. We'll be outside the church, on the steps, singing. And when the whole world is watching, we'll march up the steps and into the church. And then we'll refuse to leave. And PANN can't do anything violent to throw us out, because the cameras will be there and if they try anything then their whole peace and love B-S will be found out to be exactly that. Then, when the clocks do tick over and nothing happens—there is no giant quake, the holos don't come to life, all that—we'll take control of the sound system and oust PANN from the church and we'll be back at the heart of it all.'

'Like a target for people's fury,' said Jonah.

'No. PANN will be the target because their promises will come to zilch.'

'I don't think you completely understand humans,' said Jonah.

'And when the cameras come in to interview us, you can tell them your PANN story. It'll work. I promise.'

'You promise.'

She smiled. 'Yup.' Her eyes shone. She leaned over and was about to kiss him when the front door burst open and Bas charged into the room and stood gasping for breath in front of them.

'Whoa!' said Jonah standing up. 'What's going on?'

'I gotta tell you,' said Bas. 'What they're doing, tomorrow night. They don't know I'm here. But some-one's gotta know.'

'What are you talking about?' said Evie. 'Here,' she pointed to an armchair, 'sit down, catch your breath.'

He shook his head. 'I have to get back. I said I was going for a walk.' He looked behind him at the door he'd just come in. 'They can't know I'm here.'

Jonah had never seen Bas afraid like this. 'Go on, then,' he said. 'Say what it is.'

'There's supposed to be this huge quake, right?' said

Bas. 'Tomorrow night or the next day or whenever. And it's supposed to cut us off from the world, so we can build a New Nation.'

'We heard,' said Jonah. 'So?'

'So they're not going to trust that a quake will really happen,' said Bas. 'They've chosen a bunch of buildings around the boundary of the D-Zone and they're...' he shook his head in disappointment, or bafflement, Jonah wasn't sure which. 'They're gonna bring them down. They've planted explosives. They're gonna detonate them tomorrow at midnight.'

'Oh God,' said Evie.

'Holy shit,' said Jonah. 'I mean, seriously, holy shit.'

'I gotta go,' said Bas. The scar on his cheek was burning red from his exertion and his eyes were desperate. 'I don't know what you can do, but I had to tell someone.'

'Wait,' said Jonah. 'What buildings? And how do you know?'

'I helped them pick the buildings,' he said. 'I didn't know! They said, "What are the most quake-prone buildings?" And I thought they meant that those would be the ones to come down in the big quake, so they wanted to get people out of the way. I didn't know.'

'Well you should have,' said Jonah. 'You know what they are.'

'Jonah!' said Evie. 'Shut up. Let him talk.'

But just then the look-out, Evie's aunt, June, called

down from upstairs. 'Pilgrims! Coming up the path!'

Bas ran for the back door.

'Wait!' called Evie. 'Which buildings?'

Jonah ran after Bas into the night, but he was gone. He raced back inside to meet the trouble that was coming to the front door.

'Terrific,' said Evie 'Now we have no idea.'

There was a knock on the front door. 'I'll go,' said Evie. Jonah followed her.

She opened the door to a small crowd fronted by a tall, frowning man with a set to his shoulders that would make you think twice before crossing him. The same man, Jonah realised, who had been standing next to Bas at the rally the other night, talking in his ear.

'Yes?' said Evie, folding her arms. 'What do you want? It's late.'

He wasn't apologetic. His eyes darted all around the hallway behind her. 'I'm looking for Sebastian,' he said.

'He doesn't live here anymore,' said Jonah. 'Thanks to you.'

Evie stepped back onto his toe. 'He's not here,' she said. 'Why do you want him?'

'We're concerned for him,' said the man. 'He seemed upset tonight.'

'Is that so?' murmured Jonah. Evie pressed harder on his foot.

'He's not here,' she said again. 'And you are not

coming in.' She closed the door and leaned back on it, frowning at Jonah. 'This is bad,' she said.

18

ANNIVERSARY EVE DAWNED crisp and clear. Time was running short now. All kinds of disasters were due at midnight.

'We need help,' said Evie. 'I'm gonna go to Dirac and talk to Alphonsine. She always knows more than anyone. And, who knows, Dirac could be one of their target buildings. It's so well known, it'd make the headlines if it came down and that's what I reckon PANN is after. What are you gonna do?'

'I think,' said Jonah, 'that I'll check in with the gangs. One of them, anyway.'

Jonah made his way to a three-storey terraced house on the corner of Malt and Lowry. He was going to see Ditz Carmichael, a gangland leader whose turf included the plaza and who, they hoped, might object to plans to blow up some nearby buildings.

The front of the Ditz's place had been stripped back: no ivy, no doorbell, no fancy ironwork on the gate, no letterbox. The windows on the ground floor were barred and opaque. The whole place was tidy to the point of menace.

Jonah took a breath and grabbed the door knocker— a snarling wolf, in case visitors were slow getting the message. The knocker was loud and Jonah didn't have to try it twice. A guy the size of a small shed opened the door. He was wearing a jacket that looked like genuine leather, his head was shaved and his faultline tattoo seemed to be spreading, covering one whole side of his face in a branching black web; Jonah half-expected that it would cover the rest of the guy's face by the time he got thrown out of here. Possibly very soon.

'I've come to see the Ditz,' Jonah said.

Leather Jacket looked him up and down. 'Got an appointment?'

'No. I've got a … a warning.'

The guy's eyebrows shot up. 'That's adventurous. You better count your limbs.' But he scanned Jonah again and seemed to decide that he was no threat. Jonah was nodded inside, patted down for weapons, and told to wait right there, in a tone that had him standing unmoving for the next ten minutes. He spent most of that time convincing himself that this was a terrible mistake. If the Ditz was in league with PANN, then the whole thing would blow up, quite literally, in his face. If the Ditz decided this was scaremongering crap and chose not to do anything: same result. Jonah thought seriously about leaving. But he had promised Evie, and she would want to know what it was like in here.

The inside of the house was as aggressively tidy as the outside. It was also, without doubt, the least broken house Jonah had ever been in. Large pieces of art in bright colours hung on perfectly smooth, uncracked white walls, and the fine-grained wooden floor had been polished to a single continuous shine, the colour of dark honey. Somebody here had an unnaturally close relationship with a building crew.

Muffled voices came from down the hallway, then Leather Jacket was back, three dogs beside him. They were gunmetal grey, in sleek good health, with long, thin bodies, pointed faces and black marbles for eyes. Their black claws clicked on the floor as they circled Jonah and he opened his hands to their noses. Leather Jacket watched and after a few seconds said, 'Yeah. Follow me.'

The room he was taken to was as smooth as the hallway. More art. Deep leather chairs. A table with an inlaid top in a pattern of circles and lines. Another dog—this time a thick-haired, grey and white wolf-like animal that had been in the wars, judging by the state of its ears and muzzle. The guy sat down beside it and scratched its ears. There was a fire in the grate and the Ditz was standing in front of it.

Jonah had never been anything like this close to Ditz Carmichael, and it was intimidating, so he just nodded his head and said, 'Thanks for seeing me.'

The Ditz arched an eyebrow. She was whip thin, dressed in black jeans and an oversize black woollen jumper; her head was shaved smooth, her tattoo a simple line branching in two along her cheekbone, and she had many silver piercings—ears, lips, brows—that glinted in the firelight. He couldn't tell how old she was—not that old, he thought, except for her eyes.

The dogs arranged themselves at her feet. 'Apparently, you've got a warning for me?' Her voice surprised him. Apart from its wry amusement, it was mild and smooth. Which was strange because he could feel the fizz of her energy from the other side of the room. 'Let's hear it then.'

She heard him through without interruption or expression but a couple of times she shot a look at Leather Jacket. At the end of Jonah's account there was a long silence, then she said, 'It's going to be an exciting night, isn't it. What are you going to do?'

'Find Bas. Ask him what buildings they've targeted. Then let everyone know, somehow.'

'And what do you want me to do?'

'I just…I just want you to know. I mean, I've got no

say in how things go round here, but you…do.'

'Who else have you told?'

'No one.'

'Really? Should I be honoured?' She nudged a log of wood in the fire with her boot. 'Why me?'

What could he tell her? That her lot alone among all the gangland overlords had never had a piece of him when he delivered pizza to their door? They didn't go so far as tipping, but still—not getting pushed down the steps had its upside. He gave a small shrug. 'PANN's on your turf, I guess.'

'My responsibility, then?'

He thought it wise to be silent at that.

She smiled. 'Carlos will show you out.'

And Jonah left without any idea if what he had just done was a brilliant strategic move or a big mistake.

He headed for Hotel Dirac and met Evie coming the other way.

'It was news to Alphonsine,' she said, 'so that's a worry. She hadn't heard any whispers about it. I mean she knows that they're crazy, Phaedra and Damon, but to be blowing up buildings—she thought that was off the scale. She hasn't heard anything about where Bas might be either, but she's promised to send word to us if she does hear something. Anyway, she's got a small army of helpers who are gonna check through Dirac in case explosives have been smuggled in there. It'll take them a while, they've got a lot of rooms. How did you get on?'

Jonah told her.

'How unhelpfully cryptic,' said Evie.

'Yeah,' said Jonah. 'For all I know, she's dispatching her sidekick to Phaedra right now. We've got to find Bas.'

They headed for the plaza. It was slow going; crowds of people were filling the streets, everyone in party mode. And why not, thought Jonah. They believed that tonight they would exchange this tumble-down wreck of a place for a new beginning that was bright and fresh and magical with their beloved dead stepping back into life, easy as you like. It was a fantasy, but why not believe it for a few hours? Better than casting a shroud over your head and giving yourself up to despair.

The clouds had rolled in and the temperature was bitter. Snow on the way. The crowds got thicker the closer they came to the plaza. Impromptu bands struck up with drums, guitars, even trumpets and pipes, and people were dancing and singing in drunken delight. Jonah wondered what they were drunk on. Hope, certainly. Promises. And no doubt other more tangible substances.

People new to the D-Zone kept stopping them and asking for directions to the plaza. These people were friendly, Jonah realised, because they understood, or thought they understood, that Jonah and Evie were heading that way too. For the next twenty-four hours, everyone was of a single mind, everyone was family. This anniversary was a breakthrough coming after years of heartache and dread, of being ignored, of resilience worn down, worn thin. This time, the world would change.

Someone had sensibly roped off the holo-shrine so that the crowds couldn't stampede through it. But that meant there was a point of entry with, of course, a pilgrim standing guard and a fee to get in.

'How dare they charge people!' said Evie.

'Families get in for free,' said a young girl, over-hearing her. She was maybe ten years old, thin, grimy and not dressed for the weather.

'The hell with that,' said Jonah and stepped over the rope.

'Hey!' yelled a pilgrim. 'You have to pay!'

Evie blocked his path. 'But why, sir? Isn't this a gift? That's what the lady Phaedra said. Her gift to the D-Zone. You shouldn't be charging people for access to her gift, should you? And speaking of gifts, this young girl here clearly needs someone to gift her a coat. You don't want people to be cold in your new world, do you?'

Jonah smiled as he moved away into the holo-shrine. Evie could string out a one-sided conversation indefi-nitely and with far too much charm for her listener to feel okay about breaking off and walking away.

Even though it was daylight, the holos were a visible glimmer in the grey light. Individual features were clearly discernible, so when he got to where he was going, a chill gripped his gut. He crouched down and ran his fingers over the broken concrete. The empty space in front of him held no trace of a holo. Rebecca, Bas's mum, and Lily, his little sister, were gone. Not just switched off, either. Completely gone. The platforms that the holos were projected from had been ripped up and taken away.

He looked up, searching nearby faces but no one met his gaze. He knew now that Phaedra and Damon had found out that Bas had blabbed. And if they'd done this to the holos, what might they do to Bas? He saw a pilgrim marching towards him so he slipped away into the crowd.

He found Evie sitting on the church steps. She frowned at his news. 'Where could he be?'

'I don't know. Gone to ground.'

'Unless he's hoping for his holos to be put back, in which case he might be helping them.'

'They're not putting his holos back,' said Jonah. 'They've ripped the platforms up.'

'That's not good,' said Evie. 'Not good at all.'

They set out to walk the streets asking about Bas in every shop. They drew a blank—which wasn't too surprising: no one ever admitted to knowing anything in the D-Zone, a survival tactic of long standing. Today, everyone was edgy and busy and no one could help.

'C'mon, people, time is ticking,' complained Evie as they came out of yet another shop. 'Someone must've seen him. People walk about with their eyes closed round here.' She tucked her arm under Jonah's. 'We're going to have to ask some pilgrims.'

They went back to the plaza. It was late afternoon and the festivities were starting in earnest. Then Evie pointed. 'Look! There's the guy who came to the Matterhorn last night. Hey!' She waved her hand in the air. 'You! You there!'

The man turned towards them holding out his collection bag. 'Peace to you,' he said. He held the bag up. 'For the New Nation?'

'Uh.' Evie frowned at the bag. 'No. We want to ask you something. You came to our house last night looking for a friend of ours—Bas. Sebastian, I mean.'

The man raised an eyebrow. 'Your house? No, I don't believe so.'

'You did,' said Evie. 'You stood on my doorstep and asked for Sebastian. You knew he used to live there.'

The pilgrim shook his head. 'I don't know anyone called Sebastian.'

Jonah fished his wallet out of his back pocket and took out a note. 'Maybe this will help?'

The man held out the bag. 'For the New Nation.'

Jonah forced himself to put the note into the bag.

The pilgrim bowed slightly, said, 'Thank you,' and moved to go.

'Hey!' Jonah put a hand on his arm. 'I meant, will it

help you remember Bas?'

The man stared at Jonah's hand on his arm until Jonah let go. 'I told you,' he said, 'I don't know anyone called Sebastian. Good day to you.'

Jonah glared after him. 'You do,' he called to the man's retreating back. 'I know you do.'

'How dare he!' said Evie. 'It was him wasn't it? From last night?'

'Sure was.' Jonah turned a full circle taking in the growing crowd, people chanting and beating drums. Fires were being lit in braziers around the holo-field and on the church steps, and the holos were starting to glow in the darkening day. 'Where are you, Bas?' He was feeling sick about this.

'What would be really helpful about now,' said Evie, 'would be for the Ditz and her people to turn up in force for a showdown with PANN.'

'Yep,' said Jonah. 'Too much to hope for. Listen, when the Ditz, or Needle or Dirt Drever or any of that lot disappear someone on the quiet, what do they do?'

'What?'

'They deny all knowledge, right? Of ever knowing them—the victim.'

'What are you saying?'

'PANN found out that Bas talked, that's pretty obvious. What if they've made him disappear? And now they're deflecting attention by denying they ever knew him.'

'Oh, God!' said Evie. 'Made him disappear?'

He looked at her. 'I don't know. He was useful to them because he's spent half his life scrambling round this place. So they used him to find the buildings that'll be easy to bring down. But now he knows too much, right? Safest for them if he just vanishes. I think the other reason they chose him is he's a kid with no family, no one's got his back. He's deniable. They think they can make him disappear because who would care?'

'But he's got us,' said Evie.

'He's broken with us. They made that happen.' Jonah hesitated, then went on to the worst bit. 'Suppose you wanted someone dead but wanted to be able to deny you'd killed them, because you're all about peace and love, what would you do?'

She stared at him, then said softly, 'I'd put him in harm's way.'

He nodded. 'You would, wouldn't you. Like in a building that you knew was coming down. Jesus, Evie. Would they do that?'

There was a commotion nearby and a parting of the crowd on the edge of the plaza. Through the gap came a team of people bearing sound and camera equipment. In their midst, like royalty, walked Brett and Bev, the megastar hosts of the Glimpse Show.

'Come on!' cried Evie. Let's make a noise about this.'

19

THE LIST OF things that Shikha was not allowed to do was much longer than the list of things she was allowed to do. Under no circumstances was she to go within hailing distance of Mr Miller or Ms Fletcher, Brett and Bev, that is. She was not to go near any camera, drone or piece of sound equipment unless specifically instructed by one of the tech staff. She was not to get in the way of the security staff. She was not to ask questions, offer advice, take photos or use her phone. She was to carry, without comment, whatever bag or piece of kit was handed to her.

But no one had said anything about talking to the locals. When she saw Evie and Jonah coming through the crowd she waved and beckoned them over. 'What do you think?' She could feel a ridiculous grin coming on. 'Pretty great, right? I finally made it to the business end of the outfit. There's no stopping me now.' She paused and studied their faces. 'What's the matter?'

'Do you think you can get us in front of a camera?' asked Evie.

Shikha looked at the team buzzing around Brett and Bev like bees at a honey pot. 'To be honest? Not easily.'

'What if the choir occupied the church and refused to leave?'

Shikha's eyes opened wide and she smiled. 'Well, maybe for that.'

'Good,' said Evie. 'Let me get them together. They should be here by now.' She went off to find her people.

Shikha turned to Jonah. 'What's up? You still hoping to expose the con in the cult?' Before Jonah could answer, Morgan was looming over her with a list of instructions that began with finding Ms Fletcher's make-up case and taking it to her, and ended with being forbidden to chat with the locals.

Which is how Shikha came to be standing nearby when Brett and Bev did their first piece to camera. They were looking out over the plaza from the top of the church steps. Brett checked his teeth and his hair in the mirror that Shikha was holding then dismissed her with a wave of his hand and took the microphone from another assistant. He smiled into the camera.

'Welcome one and all to our quake commemorations on this seventh anniversary! Thanks for joining us—you're in for an exciting evening! We're in Linden Plaza, right in the heart of the Demolition Zone. We're here to talk with locals and with the founders of the movement, People for a New Nation, the enigmatic brother and sister, Damon and Phaedra. They've been riding a wave of popular acclaim here since they delivered what they've called their "gift" to the D-Zone—the mysterious holographic quake memorial you can see right over there.'

He paused while a camera zoomed in on the holo-field and a drone flew in from the north and scanned the plaza.

Bev took up the commentary. 'Damon and Phaedra have established a base at this old church behind us, and have published a manifesto promising to restore law and order to this area which is notorious for its crime. They're promising prosperity for all. Let's go down into the crowd now to see what locals have to say.'

Shikha followed at a distance as the whole set-up moved down the steps to the edge of the holo-field where Morgan was briefing a couple of locals.

Brett beamed his famous smile at one of them. 'And here's a long-time resident. You'd like to be known as M, I understand?'

'Er, yes,' mumbled the man. 'For safety.'

'Of course. And what do you think about the arrival of the People for a New Nation, sir?'

'It's fine by me,' said the man. 'City Hall doesn't care about us. Never has, never will. And good riddance to them, I say.' His voice gathered pace and decibels. 'Where was City Hall when we were being overrun by scum? I ask you! Where were they when we had bloody big assault rifles pointing out of every shitty window in this godforsaken place. Jesus H. Christ on a bike, we're fed up!' The small crowd gathering around made assenting noises.

Brett nodded, then noticed Phaedra drifting just beyond shot, smiling serenely. He hurriedly switched focus to her. 'The PANN brother and sister have been cryptic about their plans, to say the least,' he said. 'But here's Phaedra, the lady herself. Welcome.' He made room for her beside him.

Phaedra inclined her head in a graceful nod and Brett stared at her, seemingly lost for words.

'Smitten,' thought Shikha. 'Idiot.'

Bev stepped in with a polished and, Shikha thought, perfectly insincere smile. 'I believe you have an announcement to make?'

'Indeed, I do,' said Phaedra, gently. Then she turned to the camera and said, 'Today we are giving the D-Zone a new name in line with its new status. From now on it will be known as the Clearing.'

Bev nodded—Brett looked like he was still stumbling over his thoughts—and pressed Phaedra about what this meant. 'New status?'

'A transformation is coming,' Phaedra replied. 'The Clearing will be a new nation of peace and prosperity. The glimpses show us the way. That's why we have come here, to the heart of glimpsing, to usher it in.'

Bev nodded as if she knew what Phaedra was talking about. 'Tell us why this is the heart of glimpsing.'

'As everyone must know by now, glimpsing is fading in many places. But not here. This place is unique. We recognise that, and we have been guided here to welcome in a post-quake world.'

'Post-quake?' Brett stumbled in. 'Do you think the quakes will end soon?'

But Phaedra gave him her best enigmatic smile and moved away.

Brett turned to the camera. 'Amazing. Truly amazing.' He turned to a woman that Morgan had lined up and said, 'Excuse me, ma'am? What's your name?'

'Luisa. Luisa Frank.'

'And do you glimpse, Luisa?'

'Oh, yes, of course. Lots of us do.' She looked around, suddenly starstruck. 'Lots. But I'm here about something else.'

Brett frowned and Shikha couldn't suppress a smile.

'I'm here to say I'm sorry,' said Luisa. 'A million times, sorry.'

'I'm not quite with you?' said Brett. 'Sorry about…?'

174

'Well, you see. Last week I took… I took some shoes from Shoe-Mageddon. Without paying. It was wrong of me, I know. Very wrong.'

'I see. And…?'

'The holo of a boy—Anton Mora's his name—it disappeared, because I stole those shoes.'

'I don't follow. Who is Anton Mora?'

'I didn't know either! He's no relation or anything. And his family is so upset. So upset with me. Of course they are. Now I'm Public Enemy No. 1. Almost. I mean there's other people here worse than me—people who are trying to stop the New Nation. But, this is my punishment, you see, for breaking the law! Anyone who breaks the law here, they lose the holos of their family. But I don't have anyone there,' she nodded towards the holos. 'So this random child got taken. I'm so sorry! I took those shoes back. And I've apologised. And here I am apologising again. I don't want to be remembered as someone who murdered the memory of an innocent!'

'Well, thank you, Luisa. I'm sure everyone has heard your apology and perhaps a remedy will be found.' Brett turned abruptly to camera. 'And that's it for now. Let's go to a break, and when we come back, Bev will be out among the festivities, and we'll talk to some more glimpsing locals. Back soon!'

With the camera off, he turned on Morgan. 'Fuckin' hell. Don't you drop me in it like that again, you hear me? What the hell?'

Morgan held up a conciliatory hand. 'She said she was a glimpser. She didn't tell me she was a nutcase.'

'It's your job to know. Don't let it happen again. Where's hair and make-up?' He looked around and charged off towards the church.

'Well, I thought it was interesting,' murmured Shikha. She got a fierce scowl in reply and made for the church herself to avoid a further telling-off.

Evie was there conducting her choir on the steps. Shikha stood and watched, enjoying the song; it was not one she knew——something about the river Jordan. When they finished that song, the front row moved to stand behind the back row and they struck up again. Shikha could see that after four or five songs they'd be at the top of the steps. Two pilgrims on the church door were watching them sourly and Shikha wondered how Evie planned to get inside.

She was climbing the steps when Jonah appeared at her side. 'Any chance you can get me on camera? As a glimpser.'

'I can try. Come with me.' She showed her Glimpse-Corp pass to the door wardens who frowned at Jonah, but Shikha said, 'He's with me,' and they went inside.

'Thanks,' murmured Jonah.

Brett was getting his hair and make-up seen to by a fluttering assistant. He frowned at Jonah. 'Who are you?

I'm not talking to any more nutcases. Do you glimpse? I'm only going to talk about glimpsing.'

'Sure, I glimpse,' said Jonah.

'What do you glimpse?'

Jonah told him and Brett said, 'I see. Well, good, maybe we can talk to you. Do you understand what the People for a New Nation are trying to achieve here?'

'You bet I do.'

Brett looked at him, frowning, then waved the assistant away. 'Tell me exactly what you're going to say.'

'They're a con,' said Jonah. 'They stole from my family. All our savings. And tonight they're going to bring down a bunch of buildings with explosives and say it was a giant quake. And my friend—'

'Whoa, whoa, whoa!' said Brett. 'Just hold on a second there, champ. You're not making a lot of sense. Those are mighty big allegations. Can you prove any of them?'

'Of course he can't,' drawled a voice from the shadows up near the front of the church. 'Because none of it is true.' Damon pushed himself off a wall, leaned forward with both hands on his walking stick, then moved towards them.

'Where's Bas?' Jonah demanded.

Damon shook his head. 'I've no idea who you are talking about.'

'Yes, you do!' said Jonah. 'Sebastian. You roped him in with crazy promises and turned him into a pilgrim and then you used him to find the buildings you're gonna bomb tonight.'

'Whoa, whoa, whoa!' said Brett again. 'This is heavy stuff!'

'Look.' Jonah turned back to Brett. 'They're promising a huge quake this anniversary, right? Big enough to cut off the D-Zone. Big enough to bring back the dead! It's not going to happen and they know it, so they're going to fake it. My friend helped them set it up and now he's disappeared because they can't have anyone know what they're doing.'

Holy heck, thought Shikha. Brett was gazing from Jonah to Damon and back again. Then he looked at Morgan who had come in behind Shikha.

Morgan said, 'Sounds far-fetched to me.'

'Find Bas,' said Jonah. 'He'll tell you.'

'If he exists,' said Damon with a slight smile. 'This boy'—he turned the unseeing eyes towards Jonah—'has a history of concocting tales about us.'

'Really?' Brett was riveted.

'Sadly, yes,' said Damon. 'Some years ago, he came to us and asked us to heal his mother—head injury, if I recall. From the first quake. Sad, of course. But we couldn't help; it was too serious an injury. He's never forgiven us for that. There's a lot of grift in this place.'

'Sure there's grift!' Jonah was shouting now. 'It's all yours!'

'And as for the rest of it,' continued Damon, 'pure nonsense. There is no—what was that name? Bill?'

'Bas,' said Jonah savagely. 'You called him Sebastian. Where is he? What have you done to him?'

Shikha stirred and began, 'I've met—' but Morgan turned on her a look of such menace that she stuttered to a stop and before she could gather herself to speak again he had taken her by the arm and escorted her to the door. 'Stay out of matters that don't concern you,' he hissed in her ear and deposited her outside. 'Don't let her back in,' he said to the door wardens. She rubbed her arm where Morgan's grip had bruised it. In the plaza below, the crowds continued as jubilant as before and on the steps Evie's choir was harmonising beautifully.

Then the door opened again and Jonah was thrown out, still shouting, 'Where is he? What have you done to him?'

20

JONAH HAMMERED DESPERATELY on the church door, then turned and slumped against it. 'Stupid.' He banged his head back against the wood. 'Stupid, stupid, stupid.' He saw Shikha gazing at him and said, 'I thought they'd want to know.'

'And they don't.'

He scanned the plaza and blew out a breath. 'No. They don't.'

'I'm so sorry,' said Shikha. 'I tried to tell them I knew Bas was real but I was too slow. Not that they'd have believed me.'

They went down to Evie. She finished the song they were on and turned to them. 'What happened?'

'I messed up,' said Jonah. 'I should have waited till I was on camera. I was trying to explain but Damon came over and...' He shook his head in disgust. 'He's in there now with the GlimpseCorp celebs. He's never heard of Bas, apparently. And what's-his-name—Brett— believed him.' He swore and took a deep breath and said to Evie, 'I'm pretty sure it's what we thought.'

'What is?' asked Shikha.

Evie frowned and Jonah said, 'What I said in there about bringing down buildings: Bas helped them set that up, and now they're denying he even exists.'

Evie said, 'They're going to blow up a bunch of buildings and they need to dispose of all evidence. And that includes Bas.'

Shikha blinked at her, wide-eyed.

'I'm going to find him,' said Jonah.

'How?' said Evie. 'You don't know where to look.'

He frowned at her for a moment, considering. 'I think I might. Half an idea, anyway.'

'What do you mean? I don't like where this is heading.'

'Come on. Let's get away from here.' They walked down the steps to where the choir was humming in quiet harmony and Jonah told Evie and Shikha about the glimpse game.

It had been Bas's idea, of course. It had started as an attempt to wake Jonah's mother from her stillness by retrieving some precious possessions from the family home and giving them back to her. To do that—this was typical Bas—they had to break into the quake-damaged, off-limits house. They had to do it in secret because 'off-limits' was something their parents were strict about, and they had to do it without being hurt if a quake struck.

'We can go in there,' said Bas, 'because you've got this built-in warning system that a quake's coming and we can get out before it hits!' He had sat back then, impressed with his own genius.

Jonah had been less impressed. 'But I don't get every single quake.'

Bas wasn't going to be put off. 'You get the big ones, though, right?'

That first break-in had gone fine, although Bas had been disappointed that there'd been no quake in the middle of it to prove his brilliant scheme. Back with his mother, Jonah had laid a bright handful of beads and bracelets and rings in her hands. He'd placed a string of green glass beads around her neck. He put a bangle of twisted gold threads around her wrist, then a thin gold ring on her index finger and he grabbed the hand mirror he'd found on the floor by her dresser and held it in front of her. 'You look beautiful.'

She had stared with sad, dull eyes. Jonah sat for a long while holding the mirror for her, just in case, until he saw that she was looking out the window instead.

After that first foray, Bas had decided that they had to make it more exciting. He suggested they find out where the biggest, most quake-prone buildings were. 'That way,' he said, 'your glimpses will really mean something. Life and death!'

Hunger had driven them, and curiosity, and boredom. They started out looking for abandoned stuff that they could repair and sell, but they ended up doing it for the thrill of beating the quakes. Over the years, they settled on a few favourite places that they visited repeatedly: the brickworks, the cinema, the concert hall, Hotel Dirac and the train station. Jonah had drawn a line at venturing down into the subway despite Bas's entreaties that it would be the most exciting place of all. Jonah knew that the only thing he would feel if he was inside the earth during a quake was horror.

They made sure they had an escape route from every building because Jonah's glimpses sometimes hit him so hard that Bas had to almost carry him out. They were accurate, though, every one of them: hard on the heels of each glimpse, a quake.

And now, Jonah was going to resurrect that old game. But this time there'd be no Bas to get him out before the walls fell in.

'You were mad,' said Evie when he finished explaining. 'I want to go with you.'

Jonah shook his head. 'What about the choir? Don't you have a plan?'

'What about being in the path of collapsing buildings? What kind of plan is that?'

'Done it before. And look, the explosives might not even work. If they're going to try and detonate them remotely, they need decent cell reception, and they won't have that.'

'But can't you call the police?' asked Shikha.

'Tried to,' said Jonah. 'Went to the Ditz.'

Shikha looked confused.

'Local gangster,' said Evie.

'No, I mean the actual police,' said Shikha.

Jonah snorted and Evie said, 'Well, the last time I saw a cop in the D-Zone was when one of those gangsters, Rocco, staged a coronation for himself here in the plaza, called himself mayor or something. He was taken out in the middle of his big speech by one of his rivals.'

'Taken out?'

Evie formed a gun with two fingers and fired it.

'Oh,' said Shikha.

'That brought in a trickle of cops from downtown; they stuck their noses in, like they were rats twitching their whiskers at the smell of some new dead thing, and they ran around for a bit, but after a day or two they shrugged, like they do, ticked the OI box on their score sheets and went home.'

'OI?'

'Only Illegals,' said Jonah.

'Oh,' said Shikha again.

'Even if they showed an interest tonight, it'd be next week before they got here,' said Jonah. 'I have to get going if I'm going to find him.'

Evie took his hand in both of hers. 'Where will you go?' Her voice was strained and anxious. 'Tell me exactly and in what order.'

'Okay,' said Jonah. 'You already went to Dirac and warned them so that's taken care of. The rest would be brickworks, cinema, concert hall, train station.'

'Subway?'

Jonah shook his head. 'We never went there.'

'Good. Promise you won't go there?'

'Believe me, I promise.'

'And promise something else. At 11.30 tonight, you head back here whether you've found him or not.'

'11.50.'

'11.40, at the latest.'

'11.45 it is. See you then if not before.'

She scowled and kissed him lightly on the lips. 'See you then.'

None of them noticed Morgan watching Jonah go, or heard him when he turned to a techie standing nearby and said, 'Put a drone on that kid.'

21

JONAH WATCHED THE bright arc of the sun dip behind the mountains. The western sky flared orange; it was just gone six o'clock and his daylight was fading fast. He flicked his torch on, then thought better of it.

The silhouette of the brickworks was vast and dark against the sunset sky. Deserted factories like this had been catnip to Jonah and Bas in the early quake years. The grounds outside were never anything much—piles of rubble and smashed glass—but inside, giant machines lay like fallen dinosaurs and the boys' shouts bounced off wide walls and high ceilings. Jonah knew this place well.

He walked up to the huge doorway and put a hand on the doorframe. He could have sworn he felt a tremor in it and snatched his hand away—best not to think about that. Inside, the roof was broken because a hefty length of kiln chimney, which was originally double the height of the building, had smashed through it in an early quake and now lay in a thick layer of dust and rubble across a tangle of grinding and cutting machinery; the concrete floor was a cobweb of cracks and the smashed-up bricks.

There was just enough daylight left to see across the interior towards the kiln—a low arched tunnel deep inside the building, with firing rooms on either side. Suddenly, in the fading dusk light, he thought he saw Bas. Not the Bas he was looking for, but eleven-year-old Bas, running through the shadows, stopping at the entrance to the kiln tunnel and looking back, fired up, panting and laughing. *C'mon! Race ya!*

Race ya. To the end of the kiln tunnel and back, right? That's how it had been when they'd played this game as kids. The point hadn't been to win. The point had been to test Jonah's glimpsing against the risk of being flattened in the next quake. The point was the wild-eyed, heart-pounding, breathtaking thrill of it. Jonah didn't love that heart-in-mouth terror the way Bas did. He lived with the closeness of the quakes all the time, sometimes like a shadow at his back, sometimes a quiver in his mind. Never far away.

Now he reached for some of that against-the-odds belief. Ahead of him, the young Bas was waiting. *What's the matter—ya legs painted on?* This had been Bas's mum's insult of choice for laziness. Jonah almost smiled. He stepped inside.

He licked his lips, tasted dust. The wind whistled through cracks and gaps. The place stank of old clay, damp moss and nesting animals. He trod carefully, conscious of the weight of the ruined roof above him. He'd been told once that the kiln chimney was not done with its collapse, even after all these years, that each brick that fell made the ones below less stable. He was almost afraid to call out for Bas as though just the sound of his voice could bring it all down. And who else might hear if he did? That's why he wasn't keen to switch on his torch. What if someone was here to guard the explosives? He stood still and listened hard.

If Bas was here where would he be? The question reminded him of his own mother who, if she'd lost something like a set of keys, would walk around the house saying, *if I was a set of keys, where would I be?* He shook his head to clear his thoughts. The ghosts, both living and dead, were out in force tonight.

He followed his memory of Bas towards the low arched entrance of the kiln tunnel. The shadows were too dark to see through now so he risked his torch. A quick flash into the tunnel. Nothing. No pile of explosives. No Bas.

The brick-lined tunnel roof was low—Jonah reached up and touched it and mortar crumbled above his fingers. There were a dozen firing rooms down the sides of that disintegrating tunnel; he knew they were crammed with bricks and rubbish with no room for anything else, but he wanted to check. He walked along the tunnel, peering into the firing rooms, flicking the torch on for a few seconds to scan each one. He called, 'Bas? You here?' into each separate darkness and heard nothing back.

One time they'd found a dog with six newborn puppies in one of these rooms but when they'd come back a few weeks later the little family was gone. Another time, a glimpse had come to him, right here in the tunnel—the first one he'd had while playing this game. It had been a bad one, doubling him over gasping and sick and he'd been so scared that he'd cried, curled here on the floor, frozen with fear and Bas had to drag him outside.

He reached the end of the tunnel. No luck. He went back into the main space to search inside all the old machinery, then he went through the offices upstairs and peered out the windows at the rubbish piled against the walls. Still no Bas.

Jonah stopped and tried to think clearly. Could it be that he was wrong about all this? That Bas hadn't chosen their old playgrounds for this new adventure? That Jonah was chasing a phantom as elusive as the image of Bas he'd imagined earlier?

Maybe. But there was one place here he hadn't searched yet.

The chimney.

Towering beside the kiln, the chimney drew air

from a channel running the length of the tunnel roof that dived underground and came up inside the chimney stack. The door was wrenched half off its hinges and lay mangled in the doorway so Jonah had to clamber over it. His heart was in his throat as he stood up inside the narrow column. He cast his torchlight around. There was a thin metal ladder going straight up. Far, far above him, dusk light peered in.

He shouted 'Bas!' and his voice came back flat and hollow. He was about to leave when it occurred to him that they could have put Bas on the factory roof. It was flat enough and broken enough that they could have lifted him onto it from those upstairs offices. The best way to check was right in front of him. He grasped a rung of the ladder and climbed, shining the torch ahead of him, trying not to think about the drop growing behind him.

About a third of the way up, he stopped, sweat cooling on his back. His stomach knotted tight at what he was seeing: someone had chipped out some bricks here and filled the empty space with a packet strapped to a phone. He peered at it closely. There were wires connecting the packet to the phone. This was it. There really were explosives here. Set to go with the ringing of the phone.

After the first shock of seeing the packet-phone contraption what Jonah felt most was relief. Finding the explosives here meant he had guessed right: Bas had picked the buildings that they had explored together when they were kids. And something else came with that relief; it was like Bas was signalling him across the distance that had grown between them over the last few weeks, telling him where else to look. 'Coming for you, Bas,' he murmured.

He looked up, wondering if there were more explosives planted above him then realised that PANN wouldn't need more; all they needed was to blow out the bricks at this level and gravity would do the rest. The explosion needn't even be a big one, and PANN could pretend it was an earthquake after all. Jonah hauled out his phone. It was a rubbish phone with rubbish battery life and it was almost useless for calls because cell reception in the D-Zone was crap, but it did have a rudimentary camera. He took a snap of the packet in the wall then climbed quickly on.

He wanted to get to the top and peer over the edge to check that Bas wasn't lying tied up or injured on the roof. Then he wanted to get back on the ground as quickly as possible. If a glimpse came on him now… he pushed the thought away. He remembered Bas climbing this ladder once and yelling to him from the top that the view was amazing but Jonah was not one for heights and he had yelled back, 'Fine. Take your word for it.' Now he climbed and did not look down.

He gained the top and the sky opened out above him. A breath of cold wind cooled the sweat on his face. Leaning over the broken rim in the darkness, he shone his torch across the roof below. The light picked out bird-shit and rubbish but that was all. No body. No Bas.

Here on the chimney's rim, though, was something that didn't belong. An antenna. Put here, Jonah realised, to catch and transmit a signal to the phone below. He could almost hear Evie shouting at him to hurry up and get out and leave the brickworks to die, tonight, in a cloud of dust and mortar. But he was angry now, in fact he was more angry than afraid. A quake could take the brickworks when its time came, but he wasn't going to let PANN do it. He unclipped his pocket knife from his belt, snipped the wire on the antenna and pulled it free. A brick dislodged as he did that and dropped into the darkness beneath him. He held his breath waiting for it to smash into the explosive device on the wall and end everything right then, but he heard it thud into the ground and he breathed again.

He paused for his heart to stop banging so hard and looked around. He had expected it to be too dark up here for a view, but he was wrong. The bright lights of the city stretched northwest towards the mountains. The dull roar of traffic over there reached him on the wind. The city seemed to end suddenly in a block of darkness that was Wulfstan Wood and everything east of the wood, as if the D-Zone didn't exist. As if thousands of people weren't living here and making the best of tough times.

He could make out a glow against the clouds that

must be coming from the plaza; he imagined the holos gleaming and the brazier fires alight. And Evie on the church steps, or was she at the doors, or even inside the church by now? It would get ugly before long. He wanted to get back there soon. He took one last look and was about to clamber down when he heard a metallic whine, like a giant mosquito, coming from that direction. He peered into the night and saw a tiny light growing in brightness as it sped over the rooftops.

A drone. Heading straight for him. Had the bastards sent a drone after him? He ducked down a few steps and watched over the rim of the chimney as it approached. It had a very bright light and no doubt a camera. For a moment, Jonah couldn't think what to do. The buzzing came closer, then the drone's light turned straight at him, dazzling him, rocking him on his feet. He gripped the ladder hard and shut his eyes. When the starbursts in his vision cleared, he looked around and saw the drone floating low against the factory roof, turning slowly to survey the ruins. Then it crept across the roof to the chimney stack and began to climb.

Jonah stared at it, transfixed, then at the antenna in his hand. His brain finally engaged: he held the antenna out as far from the wall as possible and dropped it straight down, then clambered after it. By the time he was on the ground the drone had reached the top of the chimney and was shining its light down the stack. Jonah ran.

22

'C'MON, MAN, YOU gotta be kidding me!' Brett was furious with Morgan, and Shikha was watching, enthralled, from the shadows at the back of the church. She was holding coffees that she'd just trekked down to the plaza to get for Brett and Bev, so she had an excuse to eavesdrop. 'This is *my* show!' Brett thundered.

'Our show,' said Bev, quietly.

'Sure, sure,' said Brett. 'Our show. And you've hijacked one of our drones and sent it off on your own damn mission?'

'It's one drone,' said Morgan. 'You have three others. And you are more than welcome to do the commentary on this one. In fact, I hope you will. If it comes to anything, that is. It might not.'

'And what exactly *might* it come to?'

'That kid, the anti-PANN one you talked to—'

'The nutcase?'

'He's gone after something. I don't know what exactly, but if there's any truth to what he was saying—'

'About exploding buildings? Are you kidding me?'

'If there's any truth to it,' Morgan carried on mildly, 'we could break a great story—'

'We're already breaking a great story. *This here* is a great story! Useless, dysfunctional part of the city on the fast track to hell is pulled out of the shit by visionary leaders!'

Morgan shrugged and turned away back into the church. 'I'll keep you posted.'

Shikha delivered the coffees, receiving a smile from Bev and not even a glance from Brett who was glaring at Morgan's retreating back. 'Bloody middlemen,' he muttered and marched off out of the church, banging the doors as he went. Shikha could imagine him fixing on a smile as he headed for the camera team waiting on the steps.

It was nearly 7 pm. Time was ticking. Shikha could hear the choir in full voice near the top steps—they'd been creeping up, song by song but the PANN guards were still on the doors and showing no sign of shifting. There was a confrontation due at those doors sometime soon.

Shikha saw an assistant hurry over to Morgan and talk to him urgently. Morgan nodded and the two of them moved deeper into the body of the church. Shikha followed.

'...show you this footage,' she heard the assistant saying as he turned a screen on a trolley towards Morgan.

Morgan leaned in and studied the screen for a few moments. 'Really? What on earth is he doing up there? How high is that stack?' He straightened up. 'This is good. Keep on him. If it looks like he's onto something interesting we'll replay it to alternate with our coverage in the plaza, and if it gets really interesting, we'll go live. I want to know where he goes next and what he does.'

Morgan turned away, saw Shikha and frowned. 'Don't you have somewhere to be?'

'I was thinking,' began Shikha.

'Not what you're paid for.'

'If you go live with Jonah, then Phaedra and Damon will know where he is.'

'So?'

'They'll go after him. They'll send people to stop him.'

'Will they? Why? They think he's just a nuisance.'

'They do not. They know he's much more dangerous than that. And so do you. Why did you send that drone after him if you think he's a minor sideshow? Because you know he's onto something, that's why! If he finds explosives, or Bas, he can expose what they're doing. On live TV. Do you think they're gonna stand by and let that happen?'

'Well, it'll make for some great live action. I thought you wanted to be a director. Pay attention, because we're building a story here. These are the pieces: there's euphoria and revelry that's almost out of control among the people; there are the puppet masters, or in this case, master and mistress, pulling the strings to keep some kind of order; there's the build-up of hope for a preposterous and impossible event with a deadline that's closing in fast, and there's the outlier who might bring it all crashing down, or might be brought crashing down himself. All right?

'Whether I think that boy's onto something or not, we—that's you, me and everyone on the team—are here to broadcast the spectacle, and if we do it right, we'll give people what they want, which is to cheer the goodies and jeer the baddies. And if they don't know which is which until the last minute, all the more gripping.'

Shikha gaped at him. 'You are putting Jonah's life in danger!'

'And if we're very good,' Morgan went on, ignoring her outburst, 'we'll tug on a few heartstrings along the way. There's nothing people like more from the comfort of their couches than a bit of emotion on the cheap. And if they get all that, they'll go to bed satisfied and they'll tune in next time. Tutorial over. Go and ask make-up if they need any help.'

He left her staring in his wake. She turned to the

technician with the drone footage. 'Can I take a look?' she asked.

The technician looked over his shoulder at her and then at Morgan leaving. He shrugged. 'I guess.' He stood back and let her peer at the screen. 'This is live,' he said. The drone's light beam showed Jonah jogging past a wrecker's yard where cars smashed flat were stacked one on top of the other in teetering piles, then past a dilapidated building with BOOK BARN stencilled on its wall where, she imagined, thousands of books lay rotting in their boxes. Jonah was doing his best to avoid the drone light, ducking into doorways and behind buildings. Now and then he threw a rock at it but the drone was small and its operator was nimble. So far it had escaped damage.

Jonah stopped at a sad-looking building on a corner. Its sign, CROSSROADS CINEMA, was propped up against a pile of bricks. Its whole front wall was gone and rows of seats sat exposed to the weather, their metal frames facing the long-vanished screen, their padding lost to rot and rats. He worked his way up the central aisle, shining a torch down each row, peering under the seats. At the top of the aisle he disappeared into what must have been the projection room and the drone lost sight of him.

Shikha stepped back and realised to her dismay that she wasn't alone. A small circle of pilgrims stood watching the footage as well.

She hurried over to the technician. 'Can you close this down?'

'On Mr Morgan's say-so, I can.'

'Well, I'm working with Mr Morgan.'

'Nice try,' he said and moved to stand beside his screen.

Meanwhile, the pilgrims had marched off with a determination that worried Shikha. She decided it was time to tell Evie but before she got to the door, Brett came in trailing Morgan and complaining. 'If I have to hear from one more repentant sinner...' In a mock teary voice, he mimicked, 'I was only beating up some guy in an alleyway and I thought they'd give me the lock-up for a day, or a fine, but no, they took away my daughter's holo. Poor me, blah, blah. Jeez. Grow up, you people. I'm bored with this. Bev can do it. She's got the sympathy face. Where's that crazy kid we're following? Can we get some excitement out of him? Can I talk to him? Find out what he's doing?' He clapped his hands for attention. 'C'mon! Let's get to it! We've got hours to fill and I want some drama!' He pointed to the technician. 'You! Show me!'

The techie looked at Morgan, who nodded.

By the time Brett had finished viewing the footage of Jonah at the top of the brickworks chimney, Phaedra and Damon had arrived at his shoulder. As usual, he simpered in the presence of Phaedra.

'A troubled young man?' said Brett.

'A troublemaker,' said Phaedra.

'Of course.'

'An attention-seeker,' she added. 'Why are you tracking him?'

'Uh,' said Brett. 'No reason that I can think of, but it's not my decision.' He looked pointedly at Morgan.

Morgan smiled blandly. 'It's all part of the drama. He's giving us a good tour of the D-Zone and he says he's searching for a friend. That makes viewers engage—'

'But he's not doing that,' said Damon. 'He's trying to set people against us with these ridiculous accusations. If you persist with this, we'll have to reconsider letting you use this building.'

Phaedra put a calming hand on her brother's arm. 'It's not important. I'm sure people will get bored with him soon enough. In the meantime, let's keep track of him, shall we? See where he goes?' She nodded to Brett who rubbed his hands together.

'All right. Let's get to it, then.' He turned to the technician. 'We're going live.'

Morgan said, 'Put a delay on this—a minute will do. In case something untoward happens.'

'Untoward?' said Brett.

Morgan said, 'There may be some incentive for people to go after him if they believe he's a…well, shall we say, an enemy of the new nation? And then…you know…the possibility of violence…' He said this without a glance at Phaedra or Damon.

'No,' said Brett. 'No delays. I want to be right on the button here. There's no way I'm going to lag behind the crowd when midnight rolls round. We're going live. Proper live. And let's get that drone inside some of those buildings so we can keep a close eye on what he's up to.'

'You can't do this!' said Shikha from the outskirts of the gathered group. 'You're putting him in real danger!'

Brett frowned at her. 'Who is she? Who are you? Go away. We're working here.'

The circle closed her out.

Morgan waved her away. As she was about to stalk off, she heard Brett say, 'Is there a girlfriend?'

23

SHORTLY AFTER 8 pm, Jonah was standing at the entrance to the Guilden Precinct, the oldest part of the D-Zone. He was heading for the concert hall. Snow was beginning to fall and time was charging by too fast. Behind him, the D-Zone was going off like a firecracker. He could hear a roving crowd of pilgrims somewhere back there—it was so noisy he couldn't tell if it was a posse or a party. Possibly it was both. He wondered if Phaedra had sent some people to stop him finding Bas. If she had, they'd be having an easy time of it because the damn drone was spotlighting his every move, as though he was a rat in a maze. He'd thrown a few bricks at it but it was still up there, gawking at him.

He'd had no luck finding Bas in the old cinema, but he had found a small stack of explosives, wrapped like the ones in the brickworks chimney, with phone attached, in the basement where, again, a small explosion would yield big results. He'd taken a snap of it, then looked around and found a signal booster, which he had decommissioned with a brick.

Now he stood looking into the Guilden Precinct and wondered if anyone would be stupid enough to follow him in there. Guilden was treacherous. That had always been part of the thrill. Pre-quake, the lanes here were beautiful in a historic kind of way and now they were beautiful in a ruin-porn kind of way. Their buildings, once three and four storeys high, were brick painted in pastel colours with wrought-iron balconies overlooking cobbled lanes. They'd once housed little cafes and florists and jewellers and bars and second-hand bookshops and fancy craft shops; the kind of lanes where tourists and rich people liked to dawdle with their tiny, yapping dogs in their pricey handbags. Even now the buildings looked breathtaking in the falling snow with the drone light on them.

These days, to walk—or run—through Guilden was to risk the collapse of those old facades if a sizeable shake came through. It wasn't just danger from above, either. You had to watch out for broken cobbles and avoid the piles of silt that had come up through the earth and set like concrete. There were also a lot of ditches, and places where masonry had smashed on the ground. You had to dance it a bit.

Jonah had run these laneways often with Bas. Now, he was aiming for Santa Maria, a lane in the heart of the precinct where the old concert hall still stood. On a good day, it would take him about four minutes. But it was dark and the snow was falling and the drone light cast confusing shadows. He took a breath. 'Right,' he said to himself. He turned and gave the drone a one-finger salute, then he ran.

Two minutes in he was going well but suddenly, from the end of the lane, a wave came racing towards him: a glimpse, sending splinters of light and dark tumbling at him. It reached him, flooded his senses and pitched him into the whirlpool dark. In the splinters flashing past he saw moonlit snow draping bare tree branches and ice surrounding the riverstones; he fell through a blast of chilled air, seeing stars sharp in a frosty sky. Fear gripped him—it always felt world-ending, this glimpse fear.

Then he was back in Guilden, crouched on the ground, folded in half, helpless with nausea and mind-bending terror.

He staggered to his feet, clinging to the wall of a building to get himself upright. He croaked 'Quake,' aloud, out of habit, but there was no one around to hear except the drone and he didn't know if it could pick up sound. But in case it could, and in case it might do someone, somewhere, some good, he turned towards it, lifted his head and yelled 'QUAKE!' at the top of his voice.

Adrenaline was firing now. The quake could be two minutes coming, or ten. More likely two, knowing his luck—he got himself focused, started to think again.

Run.

He had to run. His body felt like lead. He ran, stumbled, fell, picked himself up, ran some more. He thought he might make it to Rippon Street before it hit. And after that? He couldn't think that far.

Then he heard it coming—and he could tell it was big. Run or hide? Run or hide? The shaking started and he was still running, so it must be *run*. He was nearly at Rippon… he was at Rippon, he swung around a corner and saw a rubbish-strewn traffic island in the middle of the street; it was as far from buildings as he could get. He threw himself at it and curled tight, pressed against the back of an old couch. Maybe he'd make it, or maybe something massive would fall his way and that'd be it. You never ever knew.

The quake roared, masonry pummelled the ground nearby, the silty sulphurous stink of it all was in his nose and throat.

And then it was gone, rumbling away to terrify people in the west of the city.

The earth settled.

Jonah let go a choked-up breath and lifted his head.

There was dust.

And shaking, but it was him that was shaking now,

not the world.

He pulled himself onto the couch and sat still, head in hands, breathing as slowly as he could. There'd be more quakes soon. That one was strong enough to breed a host of bastard offspring.

'Move,' he whispered to himself as though if he spoke too loud here he might bring down a building. He stood up, looked around and took off down Rippon Street, across to San Sebastian, and at last into Santa Maria, a quiet, tree-lined street of formerly upmarket terraced apartments. He stopped briefly to catch his breath in front of the smashed window and dark emptiness of the Evenstar Emporium and it almost made him smile because he was thinking of his mother who used to say that this place was high-class trash with added crystals. He sped on.

The concert hall was dark of course. The posters in its front windows advertised plays and music and dance for the coming season, but that season had passed years ago. Jonah peered through the glass front doors into darkness inside. A bench seat had been placed outside the doors for concert goers to wait for the box office to open, and a tree bent over it in a kind of benediction. The light of the drone shone through the branches and, looking up, Jonah stood for a moment catching his breath and watching the snowflakes drift, snagging in the branches of the tree. When his breathing had calmed, he listened for his pursuers but everything seemed quiet behind him.

He and Bas used to get into this place up a fire escape around the back but now Jonah had no time. He looked around for a brick, murmured, 'Sorry' to this lovely old building, and smashed his way in. As he did so, he glimpsed an aftershock coming and turned back to the drone to shout that another quake was on the way. Then he dived inside, hoping that the drone couldn't follow him in. He switched on his torch and began his hurried search, calling as he ran through cloakrooms, bars, bathrooms, offices, storerooms and into the performance space proper.

'Bas? You here? Please be here! I'm running out of time. Where the hell are you? What have they done with you? Hey, listen! That quake started a swarm, so if you can hear me, take cover, okay? I'll get to you. Where are you?' He kept this up until the aftershock arrived and he took cover himself under some seating in the hall. He knew he shouldn't be in here—that was the whole point of the game, wasn't it? Glimpse and get out.

He'd never been to a performance here and that had always been part of the joy of sneaking in with Bas. This place wasn't for the likes of them. Inside the performance space there were two levels of tiered seating, a buckled mezzanine, and cracked and faded frescoes on the walls and ceiling. All this looked towards a stage where a grand piano sat in a puddle of water, its lid broken under a heap of ceiling tiles and plaster. The thing twanged badly and a lot of its keys no longer worked, but Jonah had always loved to bash out a tune while Bas did the exploring.

Not now though. Now he ran up the aisles on both levels and along the mezzanine, looking for a huddled figure that could be Bas. Finding no one, he followed the logic of the previous two sites and climbed down into the storage space under the stage. Nestled in a corner he found the same kind of strapped-up package with phone attached. But that was all, and for a building this size it surely wasn't enough. He swept his torch around, peering into cupboards and behind tumbled stacks of tables and chairs. The weight of the stage hung heavy over his head. He found nothing—no more explosives, no booster and no Bas.

He crouched down, catching his breath, thinking about where to look next. His watch told him it was 9.10 pm. His heart was hammering and he could feel panic creeping near; his mind strained on its leash, wanting to race forward to the worst possible outcome. He tried to slow his breathing and focus.

Then the floorboards above him creaked.

He froze. There was only one exit—the stairs up to a large storage room backstage. He climbed a few stairs, listening intently. He could hear voices now. People were on the stage, talking quietly, urgently. He killed his torchlight and waited, trying to quiet his breathing.

The thought that Bas might be in the building somewhere that he hadn't looked made him feel sick because
he knew now that his search of this place was over. He
had to get out. He also knew that this old building would
likely come down tonight and there was nothing he could
do about that.

He was standing still, listening, and mentally ticking
off every room he'd looked in to make sure he hadn't
missed a space where Bas might be when another
glimpse came hurtling towards him, a whirling darkness
this time; it blurred his vision and knocked him backwards down the stairs. When he came out of it he was
being dragged upstairs by two pilgrims. Four more were
waiting on the stage.

He struggled but his arm was gripped tightly behind
him and twisted up his back. 'Caught you,' snarled a
voice in his ear.

'Let go!' gasped Jonah. He struggled again but the
grip was tight. He said, 'There are explosives down there.
And there might be more in the rest of the hall. Let me
go!'

'Explosives? Nice try.'

'Go and look!'

'Plant them yourself, did you?'

'What? NO! I'm looking for my friend. He's a
pilgrim, like you! His name's Bas. You could help me
find him.'

'Don't know any Bas,' said the snarl. Then the voice dropped to a whisper in his ear. 'The Lady P says sorry, but you're going to get tragically caught in the destruction of this building.'

'The fuck I am.' Jonah's weapon of choice had always been a fast getaway. When caught in an armlock, he had a repertoire of precisely one move, but he was expert at it and he deployed it now: he jammed his trapped arm into his side, bent low and lunged forward, pulling the pilgrim off balance. Then he twisted his whole body round, breaking the grip. He drove at the guy's legs knocking him down, then he scrambled free and took off.

'You got nowhere to run,' called one of them. 'The place is surrounded!'

Rooftop then. Jonah knew the high spaces here. The aftershock arrived and he muttered, 'Thank you! Keep it up!' He clambered out onto a fire escape and then onto the roof of the neighbouring building while the whole place grumbled and shook beneath him.

24

EVIE MADE IT inside the church, but Shikha wished she hadn't. She didn't want her to see Jonah in the drone's crosshairs. In the end, getting inside hadn't needed any subversive plan after all. It had happened because Brett required that they find Jonah's girlfriend and tug on some heartstrings. Evie's price for being roped in like this was that her choir come in with her. Which they did, smiling sweetly at the fury of the pilgrims on the door.

But after a moment's shocked silence when she realised what she was looking at, Evie had refused to watch the drone footage and was failing to deliver the tearful, hand-wringing anguish that Brett was hoping for. He tried quizzing her on whether she thought Jonah was disturbed and needed help, and she stared at him in disbelief. Then he asked what she would say if she could talk to Jonah right now, and she gave him a stony glare.

'Why would I talk to him? He's busy trying to find our friend. He doesn't need me in his ear. Now, would you like to hear some songs? We'll take requests.' Her expression was grim as she ushered the choir over to a corner and they began a gutsy song about freedom that almost drowned out the exhausting saxophone soundtrack blasting away outside. When the choir finished the song Shikha went over and asked Evie if she was okay.

Evie looked back towards the clutch of people around the screen and said, 'Who's idea was that?'

'Ratings,' said Shikha. 'I'm so sorry.'

'I guess they've sent people after him?'

'Pretty sure they have, yes. No one's caught up with him yet though. And he hasn't found Bas.'

'Are there many going after him? Can you tell?'

'Maybe five or six—they come into drone shot quite often. There's also a few dozen more behind them but they seem to be just following for the sake of following.'

'This is insane. Where's Jonah now?'

'He's been to the brickworks and the cinema and I think he reached the concert hall a little while ago. It's patchy, the footage, and they're only going to it intermittently.'

'Just the station to go, then. Where on earth is Bas?' Evie shook her head. 'I can't look. Will you watch for me?'

Shikha went back to peer over Brett's shoulder.

The screen showed Jonah running down some railway tracks, navigating the uneven ground as though he knew it well. A group of six pilgrims, less sure of the terrain, jogged and stumbled a few hundred metres behind him. They were moving through an industrial wasteland that included the giant collapsed tanks of an old gasworks, lines of deserted cottages and, near the station, some derailed train carriages lying rusting on their sides.

The drone climbed higher; the group of a dozen or so people who had been following at a distance now numbered many more—so many that Shikha couldn't count them. Their faces were lit eerily by torchlight and they seemed to have picked up their speed.

Jonah reached the barbed-wire fence around the station and crawled through a gap beneath a large red-letter sign warning would-be trespassers: KEEP OUT—FALLING DEBRIS.

Brett was getting poetic in his commentary. 'No trains have run from this station since Quake Day One when these tracks were buckled beyond use. Now we can see them heading off across this ruined ground as though there are still timetables to keep and people to move. But you don't need to follow them far to come to the end of the line.'

The drone lit an expanse of track that was all but buried in long grass, the winter skeletons of wildflowers and the settling snow, then turned and sought out Jonah.

He was standing inside a wire fence, glancing back along the tracks towards his pursuers. He jumped onto the deserted platform and ran towards the entrance where the double doors lay, twisted and wrecked. The drone lifted away and came back through the high, burned-out roof. Its light shone on the wide expanse of tiled floor; moss and weeds encroached, but the red and gold of the city's crest could still be seen. Tall windows in the smoke-stained walls looked out to the snow-swirling dark.

Brett was obviously enjoying his voice-over: 'Once upon a time those were famous stained-glass windows remembering the great and good of our city's past. You wouldn't know it now though...'

The drone light picked up Jonah standing in the doorway, torch in hand. He kept looking back over his shoulder, but he didn't go in.

'What's he waiting for?' muttered Brett off mic. 'He must know those pilgrims are catching up. Why doesn't he go in? Maybe he's had another glimpse. Doesn't want to go inside. Could that be it?' He went back on mic. 'Okay, folks, could be our friend here has had another glimpse. And that means more rockin' and rollin' coming up. Hope you're all okay out there. I'm told that the city's warning system isn't working right now, but don't you worry. You stay tuned with us. Like I said with those other shakes tonight, we've got our own warning system right here, and it's telling you to get ready to take cover!'

Shikha took herself to the doorway to wait for the quake. She hated the way the church building rattled during the shakes. Evie didn't seem to mind; no matter what, the choir kept right on singing. When this one arrived, the air was filled with shouted warnings and alarms from people in the plaza. On the steps a trio of pilgrims were lifting their arms to the sky and crying out into the storm of the quake. Not from fear, Shikha realised, but in exaltation.

'It's happening! It's happening!' cried one of them. 'The great quake is upon us!' Then together they chanted, 'New Nation! New Nation! Lady Phaedra! New Nation!'

When the shaking stopped Shikha ventured down to the small group. 'Do you really think this is the Great Quake?'

They looked at her, smiling and joyous. 'Of course! The old world is collapsing! We're seeing it. We're really seeing it. By midnight we will be a world apart—that's what they prophesied. A new nation will be born!'

By midnight. Shikha stopped still. She, and the others, had assumed that midnight was the trigger moment. Be back before midnight, Evie had urged Jonah, so that he'd be safely out of danger when those buildings came down. Shikha realised now that PANN wasn't going to wait until then. The new world was supposed to have arrived *by midnight.* Which meant very bad news for anyone prowling the ground floor of the stationhouse right now. Shikha checked her watch: 9.40 pm. She sped back inside.

She was in time to hear Brett whisper, 'Holy fuckin' cow! Will you look at that!' Then he switched his mic back on and said, 'Well folks, what you're looking at here is footage from one of our drones picking up some serious damage caused by this current series of quakes. This was the old brickworks here in the D-Zone, and as you can see the chimneystack has collapsed and destroyed the whole building. And then, if we go to this…' he wound his finger in the air at the technician and the footage switched to another site. 'This is an old cinema. Or was. It's disappeared in a cloud of dust and now there's a pile of rubble where it used to be. And I'm just getting word now that…yes, here it is, look at this! That fine old concert hall we showed you before the break has seen its last performance. And finally, our drone was right on site when this happened during that shake a moment ago!'

Shikha stared in horror as the train station collapsed in an enormous cloud of debris.

'Oh, no,' she whispered. 'No, no, no.' She ran out of the church and into the night searching frantically for Morgan.

She found him at last, talking with Bev and a camera crew beside the holos with a line of hopeful interviewees queueing behind them. 'They're doing it!' cried Shikha.

'They're really doing it! You have to stop them.'

Morgan blinked at her and gave a slight eye roll to Bev who smiled sympathetically. 'Literally no idea what you are talking about,' he said to Shikha. 'Go away, we're busy.'

'They're using the quakes tonight to disguise the explosive demolitions,' said Shikha.

'Again. Not the slightest idea. Besides, how could they? They'd have to know…Oh.'

'Yes. Oh. People glimpse here. And that includes people loyal to PANN. They know when one's on the way. It's easy to make them coincide with their explosions. That's what they've just done to the—'

'Well, so what? Those buildings are empty, aren't they, and dangerous? They might as well come down.'

'NO! They're not empty. Jonah's at one of them right now!'

Morgan narrowed his eyes at her and walked over to a small screen on one of the cameras showing the drone footage.

'Where is he? Is that the train station?'

'It was.'

'And where's he?'

'He was there! Please! You have to stop them. You'll be live-streaming a murder.'

'Don't be so dramatic. But perhaps a word with the wise is in order.' He smiled apologetically at Bev and moved off. Shikha tagged along.

Phaedra was standing in the midst of the holos, holding audience with her adoring fans. She turned to listen to Morgan and heard him out blank-faced. Then she shook her head. 'I'm afraid I don't know what you are talking about. We said a great quake would come, and it has; it's coming in a swarm rather than all at once but, still, it is as we predicted. I can't do anything about where some boy chooses to put himself. If he has landed in the path of the quake, that's his lookout, surely.'

'Wait!' called Morgan as she turned away. He moved close to her so that Shikha had to strain to hear. 'We've played your game till now,' he said. 'But enough is enough. We will not be party to murder. No more building demolitions, do you understand?'

Phaedra stepped away. 'It's you, my friend, who does not understand. Destiny is abroad tonight.'

'Then,' said Morgan, 'I'll have to stop you.'

'Stop me?' She smiled.

25

A QUAKE ROLLED through the basement where Shikha and Morgan had been put, none too kindly, on Phaedra's orders. The door was locked and a faint, flickering light bulb was all they had to see by. They'd argued, shouting across the room, about who was to blame for landing them there. Two of Phaedra's heftiest bodyguards had been directly to blame, but Morgan blamed Shikha for nagging him to front up to Phaedra, and Shikha blamed Morgan for asking rather than acting.

Then the quake burst on them.

Shikha was accustomed to her own quake reaction—fright kicked in deep in her gut, adrenaline surged through her body and her brain registered an underlying annoyance that, regardless of the size of the quake, it would take many minutes, hours even, for that surge to die down.

When the rumbling and shaking subsided Shikha unfolded and sat back against the wall. She felt utterly helpless. She should have gone back to warn Evie before racing off to find Morgan. But she didn't think anyone could have got Jonah out of the stationhouse before it fell.

She looked at Morgan. He was sitting against the wall opposite, rigid and straight, hands clasped tight on his knees, breath coming hard and short and fast. His face was pale and slick with sweat, his eyes stared straight ahead, and Shikha realised that she was witnessing a full-blown panic attack.

Panic reactions had been common in the early quake years, but then the warning system built on glimpses was established and life became less panicky——still nerve-wracking of course, but better by far than before. Shikha wasn't sure what to do. Usually she would try to help someone in the grip of an attack by showing them that she wasn't worried, assuring them that everything would be fine, encouraging them to pace their breathing, all that. But right now, while they were stuck here together on equal footing, an unpleasant sliver of her soul wanted Morgan to sweat.

She pretended not to notice and prattled on for a while about various possible solutions to their current predicament. She thought that eventually she'd annoy him enough to get him to break in and say something, but he gave no indication that he could hear her, or that he even registered she was still here. He'd closed his eyes and his face was still pale and sweaty but his breathing had begun to slow and his knuckles weren't as white as before.

She decided to leave him to come out of it in his own time and turned her attention to the basement. She got up and walked around it trying to find a signal. The best she could do was a spot by the door.

'Pack of bastards!' said Morgan eventually. 'They haven't even checked in to see if we're still alive down here.'

Shikha ignored him and studied her phone.

'Found a signal?' he rasped.

'Um, no.'

He glanced at his wrist and slapped it. 'Morons took my phone and my watch. What have you got?'

She held up the phone then went back to searching. 'It's not great.'

'What about your watch?'

'My watch?' She held up her wrist. 'My watch tells the time. You think on the crappy wages G-Corp pays me I can afford anything better? And even if we had your fancy watch, what d'you wanna do—call Phaedra back and ask for the wifi?'

'We have wifi! We put balloons in the sky tonight for connectivity.'

She stared at him, light dawning. 'Of course you did.

No wonder—'

'No wonder what?'

'I've been trying to work out why those buildings came down despite the rubbish cell reception here.'

'I don't follow.'

'Reception is terrible, right? I mean in the D-Zone, not just in this basement. Their chances of using it to detonate their explosives by phone should have been really low. Jonah thought so anyway. But if they had wifi, they didn't need cell reception. They must have known that there'd be wifi. How would they know that?'

'Not a clue.'

'I think that's a lie, isn't it? I think you know perfectly well. They embarked on this crazy plan because they thought it would work. And for it to work they needed a reliable connection to their explosives. And how were they going to get that?'

He shook his head and closed his eyes again, but after a while, he said, 'It wasn't supposed to come to anything lethal.'

Shikha nodded slowly. 'It's true then. PANN and GlimpseCorp, best buddies.'

'The hell they are. Did you notice where we are right now?'

'Only because you stopped smoothing the path for them. And how could you know it wouldn't become lethal? Anyone could see it had all the ingredients!'

'We didn't want that. Dead bodies are bad for business.'

Shikha laughed. 'Are they, though? You're the one that put the drone on Jonah. There's so much excitement in hunting someone down—that must be a ratings winner?'

He didn't answer.

'Well,' she said, 'your glorious connectivity is dismal down here. I'm getting buffer and more buffer.'

An aftershock rumbled through the basement. Morgan froze, then wrapped his arms more tightly round his knees and put his head down. Shikha sat down too. She studied Morgan's bent head. 'It's okay, we're not gonna die down here.'

'Know that, do you?' His voice was strained.

'Come on—' She waved the phone at him. 'Take this. Work some magic on it. Find your damn balloon connectivity.'

He took it and worked on it. After a moment, he said, 'Do you know where we are?'

'In a basement?'

'I mean what building?'

'I think it's the community hall—across from the church. It's a storehouse for night-market stuff. It's where we keep our stall, if you're interested.'

He kept working the phone, but eventually shook his head and put it on the ground between them. 'It's a crappy phone. Can't even get a message out.'

'A message? Who to? Do you think Ms Duval is gonna send a rescue party for you?'

He didn't answer. He pulled his coat closer around him, leaned his head back on the wall and closed his eyes.

Shikha picked up her phone and began her walk around the basement again, searching for a connection.

26

JONAH LIFTED HIS head and blinked to make sure his eyes were open. The darkness was total. He was lying flat on the ground and couldn't recall landing there. He felt around him, searching for his torch. His hand landed on it and he uttered a small sound of gratitude and switched it on.

He was in a storeroom at the bottom of some steps. A couple of minutes ago, with pilgrims at his back and acutely aware that a quake was on the way, he'd raced to take cover in a doorway inside the stationhouse atrium. He had been counting on the stationhouse to withstand the quake, just as it had withstood countless quakes over the years. But he hadn't been counting on the quake being amplified by an explosion, or the terrifying barrage of falling timber and masonry that had sent him tumbling down the steps.

He picked himself up, checked for damage and, finding none, climbed back up the steps and tried the door. It was shut with a solid finality.

Here he was, then, in the underground. The one place he'd promised Evie he wouldn't go.

He cast his torch around the storeroom. Creatures scuttled from the light: spiders into webbed corners, mice into cracks. This room had withstood the quakes better than it had withstood the looters—only a few of the wall tiles had been dislodged and lay on the ground in a thin dust of animal droppings, but the line of hooks for tools spanning one wall was empty, and so were the shelves filling two other walls; the room had been stripped. There was nothing here he could use to lever the door open.

He sat on a step and thought about Bas. He had failed, utterly, to find him. For all he knew, Bas was lying injured or dead in the wreckage above him. He couldn't bear that it had come to this. He couldn't bear being this useless. He put his face in his hands, fighting back tears. But he knew it was even more useless to be sitting here with his brain churning on despair; he mustn't give in to the churn. He thought about Evie. Look around, she would say. Find out what you've got, and use it.

All right. He turned his mind to the fact that he was alive and unhurt. A good start. He'd been lucky. Sometimes you just were lucky. People didn't like that idea. They said you made your own luck. Or they made a list of things that were bad luck and tried to avoid them. Since the quakes began that list had included lighting a candle before sunset, wasting fresh water, killing a spider or a sparrow (but not a rat—killing rats was a service, plain and simple), and walking under an awning.

But Jonah had seen too many good people lost to the quakes to believe you could tilt the universe your way just by thinking you could. If you were lucky one time, you prepped for the next quake, and you hoped, but you didn't expect, that you'd be lucky the next time too.

It wasn't down to how special you were.

So here he was. What came next? He could pound on the door and yell for help. But the only people out there were the pilgrims who'd followed him and they'd made it clear what they wanted. Alternatively, there were kilometres of tunnel around him. The upside of that? One of those would lead to a way out, eventually. The downside? There were kilometres of tunnel.

He'd been in the subway once in his life. With his dad when he was about six years old. He remembered stairs, bright lights, noise, the intercom voice, the jostle and bustle to get in line. He remembered the train sliding to a halt right in front of him, the squash of people clambering on board, the smell of takeaway coffees, the bright faces of kids in pushers, the wide smiles of buskers, all gently swaying as the train sped along beneath the outside world.

Now it was as quiet as the grave that it undoubtedly was, except for the drip of water into puddles on the platform and the rasp of his own sharp breathing.

He'd never been back. Why would he? He was used to a world where the earth could shrug a building off its foundations in a few seconds—you had to respect that kind of power.

He got up and walked out onto the platform. Even in this bigger space, the dark was clingy, as though the same stale air had hung there through all the quake years. He skimmed his torch beam around. A few paces away there was a drop into a black burrow in the earth. A train-sized burrow. A tunnel.

He was seriously tempted to run back up the stairs and take his chances with the pilgrims. Instead, he crouched down and put a hand flat on the platform floor. It felt cold and grimy. He closed his eyes, held still and asked permission of the people who were here, who'd never got out, the ones on the L train. They'd been going about their Saturday morning, thinking about what shops to go to and where to have lunch or walk the kids and the dog, until in one brutal instant the earth jumped sideways and buried them forever. He hoped it was quick.

He wasn't afraid of the earthquake dead. You paid your respects and you went about your business, grateful for the life you had. And so he'd never minded walking the streets of the D-Zone in their company. He tried telling himself now that the subway was no different. But he felt the dead as a crowd here, close as breath; they were standing in the tunnel, on the edge of the platform, around the tiled walls, watching to see what he did next.

He walked a little way along the platform. The roof had collapsed on what might have been a stairway up to the station above. There was no chance of getting up there. Nothing for it: he climbed down onto the tracks.

He started to jog. He didn't know where the L train had ended its days, but he hoped that it was well buried and a long way off. He couldn't shake the insistent image of a ghost train tearing around the next corner, lights blazing, bearing down on him. Ending him, right there.

Panic rising, he tried reasoning with himself. Thousands of people had been buried alive in the first big quake. Buildings fell on them and they couldn't be rescued before fire took hold, or the air ran out, or they bled to death from their injuries while huge aftershocks kept the rescue crews standing desperate on the sidelines. Jonah told himself that this was nothing like that. He was not being buried alive. He was moving and breathing and thinking: he was perfectly okay, alive and well, never mind that he was running through tunnels that were thick with darkness and the wandering souls of the dead.

He arrived at a station and could go no further. Rubble blocked the stairway out, but here the tunnel was blocked too, by a train.

He climbed up onto the platform and spent a moment catching his breath. To stop his brain from spinning away into the dark, he concentrated on the plink, plink-plink of water dripping into the scatter of puddles. He was desperate to be breathing real air again, even the smoky, never-clean air of the D-Zone. Down here the air and the dark were mired together, like a rag on his face, the rotting stink of it clogged his nose and lungs. The roof was too low and the walls were too close.

He didn't dare shine a torch anywhere near the train's windows. But if he were to reach the next station he was going to have to walk the length of this train inside its carriages. He was thinking how much he really didn't want to do this when a familiar nausea came at him. A glimpse. He crouched down, retching, his normal glimpse reaction amplified by the fear he was feeling down here. It was short and powerful, and then he was back on the platform, waiting for the quake. He looked around for somewhere to shelter. There was only one place. Inside the train.

Then he heard the approaching roar. He put scrabbling fingers into the edges of the carriage doors and dragged them open, diving inside as the quake arrived.

It crashed on him like a sudden storm, wrenching and twisting space, roaring so loud it was like all the trains that had ever been had sprung back to life and were racing down these tunnels; iron and concrete shuddered like tarp, dust showered from the roof; the puddles on the platform shook, and the train creaked like it was straining to move. Jonah had been through thousands of quakes but never like this—he'd never cowered right inside the earth as it heaved. He crouched inside the door, covered his head with his arms and gave in to the thunder of it. If now was his time, now was his time.

But now, it seems, was not his time.

It was over in half a terrifying minute.

Jonah stood up, gasping, sweating, chilled. He shone the torch back across the platform to delay the moment when he would have to turn into the carriage and see what, or who, was there. Finally, stomach sick with anxiety, he made himself look. His torch showed rows of seats. All empty.

He breathed a shaky sigh of relief. Just get on with it, he told himself. And hurry. It was late—nearly 10.30 pm and he wanted to get back to Evie before things kicked off where she was. He made his way down the carriage, hauling open the connecting door, telling himself that all he had to do was find a station with an exit back into the world above ground. And that could be the very next station. The second carriage was empty too, and the third. Two more carriages brought him to the front of the train. As he was about to climb down onto the track he glanced through the front window of the driver's compartment.

There was a body in the driver's seat.

Jonah froze.

His first thought was that the train had not been damaged, so how could the driver be dead? Stupid, he thought. How could there be a driver at all? Down here, after all these years? How long had it been here? What should he do? Who should he tell?

It was slumped over the controls and, he saw now, it was wearing a hood, which made it likely a gangland killing. He was grateful he couldn't see its face.

Then the body stirred.

Jonah jumped back with a yell.

The body straightened up, lifted its head and screamed.

Jonah's heart lurched. He grabbed onto the door handle, ready to run, wanting badly to run, then he steeled himself with a murmured stream of the worst obscenities he knew, reached out a shaking hand and plucked off the hood. A face twisted in pain stared up at him.

Jonah stared back. 'Bas!'

Bas's mouth was grazed and bloody where he'd managed to tear off some tape that had sealed his lips shut. His arms and legs were bound to the driver's chair.

Jonah put his torch on the control dashboard and peeled the rest of the tape away from Bas's face. Then he knelt and cut the cords binding him to the chair, saying over and over, 'You're okay, you're okay. We're getting out. You're okay, you're okay.'

Bas sat breathing in deep, wracking sobs and Jonah knelt beside him, waiting for him to calm. 'Can you stand up?' he said, and held out both arms. Bas half rose, then fell into Jonah. Jonah held him until his feet found the ground and took his weight, then he helped him lean back on the driver control panel.

Jonah unclipped his water bottle from his belt and offered it. Bas gulped down water, took a breath, and gulped down some more. He was shaking.

Jonah stood staring at him, ready to catch him, hardly daring to believe he was real.

'I...' Bas rasped. 'You...'

'Don't talk. Just drink.'

Bas went back to the water.

Jonah realised that he was shaking too. They stood, looking at each other for a silent moment, then Jonah smiled because other emotions were too overwhelming, and said, 'I'm out of snacks, sorry.'

Bas closed his eyes tight. His lips were raw from the tape, and the scar where they'd removed his tattoo was red and ugly.

'Are you hurt?' asked Jonah. 'You look like shit.'

Bas shook his head. 'I'll be okay.' His voice was raw. 'How did you...'

'Find you? Oh, you know, pilgrims, glimpses, quakes,

collapsing buildings. The usual.'

Bas's mouth twitched in an almost-smile, then he said, 'Our buildings?'

Jonah was starting to feel a surge of joy. 'Our buildings. You bet. I've been to the brickworks, the cinema, the concert hall and here, above ground anyway. Quake brought me downstairs. I think they've blown the whole of upstairs to smithereens.'

Bas wiped his face with a sleeve. 'I thought I'd die down here,' he said. 'That's what they, what they...'

'Forget them. We're getting out. The quakes aren't done for the night. Can you walk?'

'Yeah. I mean, I think so. I mean, I will. Is it night? I don't know how long I've been here.'

'Way too long.'

'You said it.' He stood up gingerly.

Jonah wrenched open the train door.

'Jonah?'

'Mm?'

'Thanks. For, you know, not giving up.'

'Yeah. Course. Let's go.'

27

IT WAS GETTING very cold in the basement. Shikha walked briskly back and forth, rubbing her arms to try to warm up. 'Do you think they'll let us out any time soon?'

Morgan ignored her.

She tried again with something less difficult. 'How long have you worked for Ms Duval?'

This time Morgan glanced at her. Then closed his eyes again.

'I see,' said Shikha. 'Top secret, is it?'

'What exactly do you want?' he asked.

'So, it's okay for me to answer your questions, but not for you to answer mine?'

He swore quietly. 'I've worked for GlimpseCorp from the start, from when it was a fledgling idea in Quake Year One. From before it took over the tower from some failed bank and became the most successful start-up in a generation. Satisfied?'

'See, that wasn't so hard,' she smiled at him. 'I don't even know your first name and you've probably forgotten mine. It's Shikha, by the way.'

He picked up the phone and had another go at getting a signal.

'Okay, sorry,' she said. 'I guess most people call you "sir." Please do not throw the phone across the room; that will only make it more crap than it already is, and it's the only one we've got.'

He placed it on the floor as though it was contaminated with something unspeakable. Shikha didn't bother picking up the useless thing. She asked again, 'Are you expecting GlimpseCorp to come to the rescue?'

Morgan looked ill and didn't answer. Every few seconds a tremor ran through his body.

Shikha grimaced on his behalf. 'Headache?' She knew the aftermath of a panic attack. He'd be nauseous, headachy and shivery for some time. She shivered too and, not for the first time, banged hard on the door. 'Hey! We need some medical attention in here! Hey! C'mon!'

Nothing.

She resumed pacing.

Morgan didn't move.

'Can I ask you something?' she said.

He shook his head, eyes still closed.

'If Jonah's lost under that building,' said Shikha, 'what will you do? What's your emergency get-out clause? Is it something like: Oh dear, what an unfortunate accident, here's a tiny bit of compensation for his family? Do you have insurance for these kinds of eventualities?'

'He's not dead.'

'You don't know that. You have no idea. Even if he got out of the station, there are still those pilgrims chasing him. Can't you call them off? Or tell PANN to?'

'They haven't exactly listened to me so far.'

She studied him. 'Terrific.'

The phone blipped into life and they both made a grab for it.

Shikha won. She knelt down and held it at arm's length so he could see too. The drone had lifted high above the streets to show the industrial zone, the rail yard, the severed tracks, and the remains of the station-house, now a smoking ruin. The devastation was much worse than Shikha had imagined.

'Oh, no,' she whispered.

Morgan was silent.

They watched as a procession of lights appeared on the edge of the drone shot, about four blocks from the station. The drone zoomed in, showing a much larger crowd of people than before. It had acquired a drummer and people were chanting but she couldn't make out the words. They lit their way with torches of all kinds, some battery, some flaming. Most of them looked like they were having a good time, laughing and singing, but a few looked more intent and one or two looked murderous. Then someone peeled off from the margins and hurled something through a shop window.

'And now the looting,' she said. She'd walked in those streets, and looked in those small shops. They had very little worth stealing. Remembering what Jonah and Evie had said about police being occasional visitors here, Shikha wondered how out of control this would get.

The drone was swooping down to street level. It hummed along at speed, winding through the lanes near the train station. Brett's voice came over the visuals. 'Well, it's all going down here, folks. There's a parade. There's the station destroyed—'

Then the buffering was back. Shikha cried, 'No, no, no!' and stabbed helplessly at the screen but it remained resolutely frozen. She swore and sat back on her heels.

Morgan murmured, 'He's a fool.'

'What? Who?'

'Brett Miller.' He shook his head and dug his palms into his eyes. 'Thinks he's still in charge. Anything for a profile.' He pushed his fingers through his hair and stopped with his head in his hands. 'If that's a parade, I'm my aunt Nora.'

'What did you expect?' asked Shikha.

He looked at her, a level stare in the shadows. 'I

expected that we'd manage it, with PANN. Kerryn said she had a good relationship with Phaedra. And a contract, for God's sake. It was meant to be a spectacle. A celebration of the holos and of surviving seven years of these fucking earthquakes. I expected a bit of stupid nonsense about a new world and that we'd all go home happy in the morning after a good night's entertainment. I did not expect PANN to create a mob. I did not expect—do not expect—to lose that kid.'

Shikha glared at him. 'Well, it's probably too late for that now.' He looked away. She stood up and banged hard on the door. 'Hey! Let us out! C'mon! Let us out!' She put her head on the door and wanted to cry. Then she heard steps on the stairs, the lock turned, the door opened. Shikha stood blinking in surprise at the man who stood in the doorway. He was so huge and square that he was practically a monolith. A serious-looking gun was slung across one shoulder and a knife was sheathed at his belt. His faultline tattoo covered most of his face. A chill came off him as though he'd brought the snow inside. He did not smile. 'You,' he said to Shikha. 'Come with me.' He looked past her to Morgan. 'You too.'

'You have got to be kidding,' said Morgan, but he got to his feet.

The monolith did not look like he had a funny bone in his body. He regarded Morgan with an unpleasant stare, then said, 'You are under the protection of Ditz

Carmichael. Count yourselves lucky. Could be worse. Follow me.' Then he turned and walked back up the basement stairs.

28

'HELL OF A thing,' Jonah said to a man in the crowd who stood surveying the damage to the stationhouse.

'Sure is,' he said. 'That's why we're gonna get the lowlife responsible.'

'You're what?'

'That drone up there?' said the man. 'It's tracking the kid. Every building he's been in—' he made an exploding gesture with his fingers—'down it comes. He's setting explosives. You watch the Glimpse Show? We're going to find him and take him in.'

'No, no!' A woman nearby broke in. She was wearing a pilgrim tunic under a fur-collared coat. 'You've got that wrong. It's the quakes that are bringing down these buildings. It's how the new world is coming through.'

The man smiled and shook his head. 'You reckon? And I say it's a kid planting explosives.'

'I'm telling you,' she said, 'it's the quakes! What would the Glimpse Show know, anyway? They have no idea what's really going on. You might as well listen to City Hall.'

'Then what are you doing in this crowd?' asked another man.

'We're touring the sites!' she beamed. 'Bearing witness to the quakes, of course. It's so exciting!'

'You're not from round here, then,' muttered Jonah.

Another man, leaning in to listen, said, 'I thought we were here to patrol the boundary of the D-Zone to keep outsiders from coming in. City Hall's gonna send police and troops to take over this place and we're gonna stop them.'

The first man laughed. 'It's all a good time, yeah? And you can collect a few souvenirs along the way.' He turned to Jonah and Bas. 'What about you? Why are you here?'

Bas, buried deep in his hoodie, didn't answer, but Jonah said, 'We're tagging along. Seeing where it goes.'

The guy gave a nod. 'Souvenir hunting? There's a few shops around here you can check out—security's rubbish in all of them and in plenty someone's done the entry for you already. I mean it's crap mostly, but it's free.'

Jonah grunted an assent and turned away. He knew the shopkeepers down these streets. It would cost them months of their meagre incomes to get their smashed windows fixed and their stolen stock replaced. He kept his head down and drew Bas towards the back of the crowd.

Jonah was rattled by this competing strand of news that apparently it was him and not the quakes bringing down these buildings. It made no sense unless, perhaps, you were Brett trying to rev up your audience while still showing you weren't buying the PANN mystique. And then there was the rest of what the man had said. Every building he'd been in was gone now. They'd been like old friends, those buildings. Deadly old friends, but still.

'Are you okay?' he asked Bas. 'Can you walk?'

'Yeah, sort of. Where are we going?'

'We're going to find Evie. We're leaving this lot to go to hell.'

The last of the crowd's stragglers trooped past them and it was like they were suddenly breathing clear air again. Bas lifted his head, closed his eyes and let some drifting snowflakes land on his face. After a moment he said, 'The station house?'

'Destroyed. Bastards.'

'And the rest?'

'Gone too. That's what those guys in the crowd were saying. I mean, I saw the explosives, so I kind of knew it was coming. It still stinks, though.' He told Bas about his search of the brickworks, the cinema and the concert hall. 'We warned Alphonsine about Dirac. Was Dirac one of them? We guessed it was.'

Bas nodded. 'Yeah. God, the people in Dirac! I would never—'

'Alphonsine will have handled it. Were there any others?'

'Those were the ones I told them about,' said Bas. 'Quake-prone and spectacular is what they wanted. And I delivered. What a pushover I turned out to be.'

They walked in silence for a while then Jonah said, 'I climbed that frigging chimney, you know.'

Bas laughed then grimaced at the effect on his grazed lips. 'It's a view.'

'It sure was,' said Jonah.

They walked on, then Bas said, 'I didn't even wonder why they wanted them to be spectacular. I thought, Great Quake, big dangerous buildings—they'll want to get people out of the way. Jeez, I messed up so bad. They must've seen me coming from a long way off and thought, *Great, just the sort of idiot we need.*'

Jonah shrugged. 'You and me both.'

The streets were nearly empty now, the sounds of the crowd a distant rumble. Jonah wished they could hurry. Midnight was about an hour away, and he was worried about Evie—at this rate it would take them half an hour to get to her. Maybe longer because Bas was fading fast. They stopped at Cosimo's 24 Hour Goods and Groceries and bought some chocolate bars. Cosimo was sweeping his front window off the pavement and greeted Jonah with a sigh and a shake of the head. 'Hoodlums! The lot of them.' He gestured inside to shelves swept clear and boxes of vegetables overturned.

Jonah handed over some cash.

Cosimo smiled. 'A man who pays for his goods! Thank you, Jonah.' He frowned at Bas. 'Looking a bit rough tonight?'

'Had a tough day. He'll be fine.'

'Take care, now.'

'You too. Sorry about the mess.'

They walked on, Bas a little brighter now. 'I guess I fell for it hard, didn't I? Should have seen it was all a trick.'

'They told you you'd get your family back. That's strong stuff.'

Bas said, 'It's like, we made it through the worst, right? Mum and Lily and me. And we thought we'd got out of it, safe, and then… then one shake and they're gone.' His voice cracked. 'It's not right.'

'That's for damn certain.'

'Do you think it's all part of some plan?'

'Nope.'

Bas glanced at him. 'You sound pretty sure.'

'Because I am. Someone came at Dad and me once, after church, with: *Oh, it's all part of God's plan*. And Dad was having none of it. He said, "You think God decides you get to die now and your next-door neighbour doesn't? All the people that died, they had as much right to make it through as you or me. We were lucky, that's all.'"

Bas walked in silence for a while, then said, 'But it's not just luck, is it. Because if that department store had been in the city centre, or in the west, it would have been pulled down by now, or at least had decent fencing. Then people wouldn't have been walking near it when the front fell off. And they'd still be here.'

29

SHIKHA AND MORGAN stood in a dimly lit corner of the community hall surrounded by the detritus of the night market. The man who'd let them out stood behind them. In front of them was a woman that Shikha decided must be the Ditz Carmichael whose protection they were supposedly under now. She didn't know whether to be relieved or very worried. The woman was dressed in black leather and her many silver piercings glinted in the shadows. Like a knife blade in its sheath, thought Shikha, who was feeling hyped up and emotional.

Morgan appeared to be feeling neither of these things. 'Who the hell are you?' he said.

The woman lifted an eyebrow. 'I'm the person who let you out of the basement.'

'Why?' demanded Morgan.

'You can go back in if you like.'

He sighed. 'No, I mean, thank you. You must have your reasons?'

She smiled. 'I'm tired of listening to your man over there.' She nodded towards the church. 'He's in thrall to this cult and it's going to end badly. I want you to go over there and shut him up. Or at the very least, get him to find an angle on this whole sorry business that's not entirely bullshit. Do you understand?'

'I think so,' said Morgan.

The woman checked her watch. 'Good. It'll be midnight soon and who knows what they've got planned for that. On you go. Carlos will go with you. Thank you, Carlos.'

Morgan nodded and moved towards the door, but Shikha hesitated.

The sharp gaze of the woman fell on her. 'Well?'

'I, uh, I wondered,' Shikha stammered, 'I wondered how you knew we were in there?'

'Did you?'

'Uh, yes.' Shikha knew she was riding her luck. 'Does letting us out mean you're against what PANN is doing here?'

The woman sighed, and Shikha realised, not for the first time, that there was a lot going on here in the D-Zone that she had no idea about at all.

'I take an interest,' said the woman. 'But also,' she frowned, 'I liked the concert hall.'

Morgan, waiting at the door, cleared his throat ostentatiously.

'All right, all right,' said Shikha. 'Coming.'

Outside, the holo field glowed ghostly in the thinly falling snow; it was astonishingly beautiful. But the crowd was not beautiful. The crowd was huge and agitated. Fires were burning in rubbish bins, drums were beating, a chant had begun: 'QUAKE! QUAKE! QUAKE! QUAKE!' A wild anthem soaring across the plaza summoned everyone to the holos. People had come for a miracle and now was its time.

Shikha shot a look at Morgan who was stalking along beside her, hunching his shoulders against a flurry of snow, his face set. She wondered if he might try to cut loose, to get out and leave them all to the chaos that would surely follow the arrival of midnight.

She decided to distract him. 'Oh, look!' she pointed to Bev deep in the holo field, still interviewing, still with her sympathy face on. Shikha looked around for Brett and spotted him on the church steps, doing a piece to camera, gesticulating widely to take in the whole plaza. 'Of course,' she said. 'He has to be the centre of attention.'

They hurried down the steps of the hall followed by Carlos, the monolith. Morgan hesitated on the edge of the holo field. 'We need Bev out of there. I don't like the way this is going.' He stepped among the holos and Shikha followed. Every holo had its visitors tonight and they'd brought all manner of offerings: candles and winter greenery, stuffed toys, treasured clothes and jewellery, polished stones and hunks of rock. A subterranean murmur of prayers and songs troubled the air beneath the shrill of the saxophone.

Then a voice began booming a countdown: 'THIRTY MINUTES! THIRTY MINUTES TO MIDNIGHT!' The crowd stirred and murmured, like an ocean shifting in its depths.

Bev had just finished talking to twin girls who were with their father at the memorial holo of their mother. 'Sweet,' said Morgan to Bev. 'But now it's time to go.'

'Just when it's about to get interesting?' said Bev.

'Let's not be here when it does,' said Morgan.

'Two more interviews,' said Bev. 'Then we head back.'

Morgan shrugged. 'It's your funeral.'

'TWENTY-FIVE MINUTES! TWENTY-FIVE MINUTES TO MIDNIGHT! The crowd on the edge of the plaza whooped, but the people in among the holos held still in their own kind of limbo.

30

JONAH AND BAS stepped among the ranks of shining holograms. Jonah figured it was the safest place to be because they could lose the men who were after them in the lights of the shrine. Evie and the choir were no longer on the church steps. He knew it would be too much to hope for that she'd gone somewhere safe. Maybe she'd done what she planned and got the choir into the church, which made them sitting ducks when the crowd went mad with disappointment at midnight. Jonah thought about running up the steps and bursting in but there was the small problem that as soon as he turned up there the PANN siblings, or GlimpseCorp, or all of them together, would hold him for planting explosives. Evie would expect better tactical thinking than that.

He checked on Bas, who was looking forlornly at the holo faces, and he recalled the kindness of Bas's mother and the gentleness and joy of Lily, now gone from the plaza as well as from the world. His heart ached for all of them.

The saxophone was shrill and nerve-jangling, and whoever had the megaphone had gone to a minute by minute countdown. A swirling, blustery snow had started to fall again. Jonah felt cold to his bones. He guided Bas towards the steps where he could see Art standing at his usual place with his beloved Lucia. Jonah was hoping he could leave Bas with Art for safekeeping while he kept searching for Evie.

As they walked among the holos he asked everyone he could about Evie. Some of them remembered hearing the choir on the church steps but no one could tell him when they left or where they might have gone. Most of the people he was talking to showed no interest in PANN or its promises. They were there to honour their dead and were inviting Jonah and Bas to join them.

The mourners felt like kin tonight. Jonah stopped to talk to Vern and Rose, who gave away the entire contents of their fruit and veggie shop the afternoon of Quake Day 1—they were here with the holos of their lost kids, Maggie and Jack. Frederica was here in front of her husband Monty—Freddie had sat with Jonah's mother all through that afternoon while they waited for the medics who never came. And Albert and his son Jem were waiting here with the holo of their lost Rosanne;

they'd heaved rubble that day alongside Jonah's dad, working frantically until darkness fell and then they'd rigged up lights to carry on, and they'd worked for hours until no more voices came from inside the ruins. There were so many, thought Jonah.

All these people here right now with their big weary hearts, they were always on hand to help, no matter their own exhaustion and the weight of their own sadness. It was these ones, and, Jonah had no doubt, thousands of others he didn't know, who'd held the D-Zone together that first day and in the days after. They weren't all here, of course. A lot had died in the seven years since, some in buildings falling in aftershocks, but more, he knew, from exhausted hearts and minds.

Then, from the corner of his eye, he saw a holo move.

Fear uncurled in his gut.

The holo was between him and the church steps and it had definitely moved. 'Did you see that?' he said to Bas.

'What?' Bas looked up from under his hood. 'No?'

'Come on!' Jonah ran, ducking and weaving through the crowd, trying to follow the glowing figure. There were so many holos—they were a blur of light and it was hard to distinguish them in the falling snow. He lost the moving one, then found it again. It had stopped at the bottom of the steps. Jonah and Bas were ten metres away from it when it turned and looked at them.

Phaedra. She was dressed in a hooded cape of flowing

white with pale blue lining and she was holding a glow globe in both hands. Its pale radiance shone through her cape and on her face so that she seemed to be lit from within. Then she began to walk up the steps towards the church entrance. At the top, she stopped and turned back to face the plaza; she lifted the globe towards the sky, like an offering.

'What's she doing?' Bas whispered.

'No idea,' said Jonah. The glowing light and the snow and her place on the steps made Phaedra look taller than ever. But that's all it was; a trick of the light. Still, she scared him and awed him, like she always had.

'FIFTEEN MINUTES! FIFTEEN MINUTES TO MIDNIGHT!' Jonah drew Bas to stand beside Art at the bottom step. Bas reached out and touched the light that was Lucia and his eyes filled with tears and Art gave him a sad smile. Above them, Phaedra was looking across the crowd, her face lit with satisfaction. Suddenly Jonah couldn't stand it any longer: Phaedra and Damon had used the D-Zone and its brokenness to take money from people who had little, to offer fake promises to people who had lost hope and to build themselves up as the answer that everyone needed. Bas had nearly died for that plan. And Phaedra hadn't even noticed that Bas was standing right here. Jonah was sure she wouldn't recognise him because, to her, he was just another gadget to deploy when needed. The whole D-Zone, people and buildings, were like pieces in a puzzle that the PANN siblings were fitting together for their own ends: money and glory.

Heart pounding, Jonah climbed two steps and called up to Phaedra. 'Hey!' His voice came out strong. 'Where is it?'

'Jonah,' called Bas. 'What are you doing?'

Phaedra opened her arms wide, letting the globe go so that it hovered in front of her. She blinked at Jonah slowly and her voice rang cold and clear across the space between them. 'Where is what?'

People stopped to watch.

'Your new world,' said Jonah. 'I don't see it.'

She smiled. 'You'll never see it. In fact,' she looked around at the people nearby and then out across the plaza to the thousands who had gathered there. '*You* may not see the morning.'

'Don't let her spook you,' called Bas.

Jonah couldn't oblige. He was seriously spooked.

'Well, well,' said a voice behind him.

He spun round.

Damon.

'Pup's found his voice.' Damon walked past him, guided by a pilgrim, and mounted the steps to stand beside Phaedra. He lifted both arms and called out to the crowd. 'Hear me! Our world cannot be transformed while deceivers stand here and challenge our truth! Are you going to let them do that? Or are you going to silence them?'

'Shit,' said Bas.

Jonah's heart hammered. 'You're a fake,' he yelled. 'All this—it's all fake!'

'What are you doing?' called Bas again.

Phaedra said, 'I'm not afraid of you, boy.'

'No?' said Jonah. 'Well, I am afraid of you. But you know what? I'm not afraid of them.' He gestured across to the people waiting with their holos. 'I know them, I know what kind of people they are. And I know that you feed off them. You…you feed off their sadness and what they've lost. You get fat on it and you don't care who you spit out and leave behind. And if that's your great transformation, I don't want it.'

He turned and walked down the steps and away, his heart still pounding. Bas hurried behind him, looking back over his shoulder. 'She's sending people after you.'

'FIVE MINUTES! FIVE MINUTES TO MIDNIGHT!'

'We're just gonna walk,' said Jonah. 'And we're gonna stay in the holos. And we're going to work out what to do next, okay?'

From the edges of the plaza, some of the crowd began to invade the holo field. People began shouting, whistling, yelling. *'Hey! Turn round, kid, let's see you.' 'Who do you think you are?' 'Turn round!'*

The sax was shrieking now and the chant of 'QUAKE! QUAKE! QUAKE! QUAKE!' went up behind them. People at their holos stood up, arms wide, to guard them from the invading crowd but they were being jostled and shoved.

'THREE MINUTES...'

'When do we run?' said Bas. 'Now? Jonah? Now?'

Something whizzed past Jonah's ear and smashed into the ground ahead of him. A snowball. Then another. Then one thumped hard into his back and he stumbled. He looked back and one struck him a glancing blow on the head. He yelled in pain and put a hand up to his forehead. His fingers came away bloody. There was more than snow in that one.

'ONE MINUTE! FIFTY-NINE, FIFTY-EIGHT, FIFTY-SEVEN...'

Jonah looked back again and saw that his pursuers had paused to join the countdown.

'TEN! NINE! ARE YOU READY? THREE, TWO, ONE. *AAAAAND...MIDNIIIIIIGHT!*'

A roar erupted from thousands of throats.

And when the roar faded, there was silence. The music had stopped.

People in the crowd paused and looked at each other. Those who were shielding their holos from the rampage dropped their arms. The drums fell silent. People ceased their partying and their chanting. Everyone turned towards the source of the silence; they held still, they waited in the falling snow.

Phaedra and Damon stood on the top step, arms raised for their big moment. Brett and the Glimpse-Corp camera focused closely on them. Phaedra started to speak but a loud burst of static on the sound system drowned her out, then came a screech of feedback, then a voice, saying: 'Hey there, people! Do you want to hear a different song? I think you do.'

Jonah looked at Bas. 'Oh, yes! Come on!' He started to run.

31

'OH, JEEZ,' WHISPERED Shikha as Evie's glorious voice lifted smoothly into the air. 'What is she doing?'

My life flows on in endless song;
Above earth's lamentation...
Through all the tumult and the strife
I hear the music ringing;
It finds an echo in my soul—
How can I keep from singing?

Shikha had watched Jonah confront Phaedra—along with, she realised, thousands and maybe millions of viewers, courtesy of Brett's camera team. She wondered what commentary Brett had offered to that encounter: something rabid about Jonah no doubt.

But the important thing was that Jonah was alive. And he'd found Bas. She felt the relief of that through her whole body. But she knew it wasn't over. There were angry people down in that crowd and they were giving vent to just how angry they were. Things were being thrown at Jonah and Bas and voices were accusing.

She turned to Morgan. 'We can't let a mob chase Jonah down. You have to do something.'

His eyebrows shot up. 'Do I? I thought we were grabbing Brett and Bev and pulling out?'

'But you said, and I'm quoting here: it wasn't supposed to come to anything lethal.' She pointed at the crowd. 'And now we have this.' The drums had started up again, and the chanting, and people were making torches from the bin fires. Evie's voice still floated over the plaza but now it competed with voices in the crowd that were raised in confusion and fury.

Morgan frowned. 'Did I did say that? Yes, all right, I suppose I did.' He closed his eyes and pinched the top of his nose in a gesture of resignation.

Phaedra was holding up her hands for quiet while Brett was murmuring into his mic as his camera operator panned across the crowd and came back to Phaedra.

'All right,' said Morgan. 'Let's see if we can calm this thing down. We need to get inside and talk to the technicians so we can get the sound system sorted for both here and the broadcast. Do you think our friend might help us get in?'

Carlos was standing a little distance behind them,

unswayed by the crowd surging around him. In fact, the crowd seemed to break on him like storm surf on a lighthouse. 'Maybe,' said Shikha. 'At least he might get us past Phaedra without being deposited back in a basement.'

'A word,' said a voice behind them.

'Ah,' said Morgan. Carlos had advanced two paces and was standing at their backs. 'The man himself. Yes? Any thoughts?'

'There is another entrance to the church building.'

'Won't it be locked, though?' said Shikha. 'Against the mob?'

Carlos gave her a pitying look. 'Follow me,' he said.

Evie was surprised and relieved to see them. She even greeted Carlos warmly. 'Jonah found Bas! And then he took on Phaedra! It was amazing. But that guy, Brett?' She nodded towards the screens on the trolley. 'Can we shut him up? He's spouting dangerous rubbish about Jonah.'

'Yes,' said Shikha. 'Exactly. Morgan's going to, er'— she looked across to where Morgan was in conversation with a technician—'say something. I think.'

'Good,' said Evie. 'The techies want to leave. They're scared about what's happening out there.'

'Aren't you?' asked Shikha.

Evie raised her eyebrows. 'Right now, I'm worried for Jonah and Bas. That is top of my mind, other stuff can wait.'

'Well, we're going to calm things down. I hope.'

Morgan was back with them. 'There's a big crowd out there. Wouldn't take much to bash down those doors and storm in here.'

'I have a plan for that,' said Evie.

'Oh good,' said Morgan dryly. 'And what's that?'

'What's in the crypt,' said Evie.

'Ah,' said Morgan. 'Of course.'

'What?' demanded Shikha. 'What's in the crypt?'

'The control centre for the holos,' said Evie. 'If anyone tries to break in here, we'll turn the light show off. That should confuse them.'

'Inflame them, you mean,' said Morgan. 'No. I don't think so. We'll try a few home truths first and see where that gets us. I'm not guaranteeing anything. You might think that when promises turn out to be dross in the morning, believers will walk away peacefully. I'm not so optimistic. But we can hope.'

Morgan commandeered Brett's camera team and mic, much to Brett's purple-faced outrage and Shikha's immense satisfaction. The crowd, volatile, uncertain and intrigued, watched as Phaedra and Damon smiled, expecting perhaps, that Morgan would be offering the simpering adulation they'd received from Brett. Then Morgan spoke to the crowd and, by means of Brett's camera team, to a much bigger audience in the city and beyond.

'Hello, everyone. I'm from GlimpseCorp, and I have a story to tell you about the People for a New Nation.' He pointed at Phaedra and Damon. 'When we found them a few years back, they were a pathetic little sect with half a dozen followers, tripping about in painted buses with bells on their toes making money any crooked way they could.'

Phaedra turned to him with an arm outstretched and shouted, 'Liar! Be silent!' She looked around for her pilgrim entourage who were standing at the bottom of the steps and gestured for them to come up. But at that moment, Carlos emerged from the church and stood beside Morgan. The pilgrims who had been on their way up hesitated then stopped, unsure about this new development. Phaedra looked momentarily confused and murmured something to Damon.

Morgan was saying, 'And how did PANN grow into the monster it is today? GlimpseCorp money, that's how. We funded the holo tech, the glow globes, the marquee, the arrival here by helicopter, hell, we funded this sound system. And why? Because, ladies and gentlemen, GlimpseCorp needs glimpses. More than that, GlimpseCorp wants a monopoly on glimpses, and you here are rich in glimpsing. But you're not going to front up to a flash corporation, not with Border Control on your case. Sending PANN to you was Step One: lure some glimpsers, make them feel safe, then channel them to GlimpseCorp.

'But that's not all. Step two was to cement control of the D-Zone. And GlimpseCorp has done this by buying the D-Zone from City Hall. That's right. They own the land you walk on. But make no mistake, they have no intention of rebuilding here. On the contrary, they want to make sure that never happens. They want you cold and hungry, they want you feeling unsafe, they want you worried about the BCB coming to your door. In a word, they want you stressed. Why? Because their research tells them that stressed and fearful people make the best glimpsers. They figure that if you get a little solace from the fantasies that PANN feeds you, well, good. It'll keep you quiet. Then they can use you in glimpse warning systems for this city—and beyond.'

He paused for a few seconds, looking out at the crowd. 'What happens next is up to you.' He wiped a hand over his face as though he was sweating despite the cold. Shikha thought he looked ill. He turned to the camera team. 'Close it down and go home. Take Brett and Bev with you.' Then he handed the microphone to Evie. 'It's all yours. Sing yourselves a happy future.'

Shikha stared at him. He looked different now. Shrunken. A bit lost. A thin man in a bad suit and ill-fitting coat who'd just thrown away his career.

Brett grabbed the mic back from Evie. 'How dare you!' he said to Morgan. 'Who do you think you are?

You're a middle-management nobody—'

'Shut up, Brett,' said Morgan. 'It's time to go. Past time.'

'I'm pretty sure you've been fired by now,' said Brett, 'so I guess you're not calling the shots anymore. Besides, I've cued up an interview with Phaedra and Damon.' He turned with a curt jerk of his head to his camera crew and made for the siblings.

Then he saw Jonah dashing up the steps and seemed to decide that this was the bigger scoop. 'Hey there!' he called to Jonah. 'You! A word! A word!'

Jonah had just caught Evie up in a big hug. Now he turned to Brett. 'If you like,' he said, and before Brett could stop him, he took the mic and walked a few steps away, holding up a hand to the crowd. 'Hey everyone! Listen!'

Shikha enjoyed the tussle she could see on Brett's face; should he attempt an unseemly struggle to get the mic back or should he stand aside, looking aloof, as if this was all part of his plan? The crowd stilled to watch.

32

JONAH LIFTED THE mic and spoke. 'Another quake's on the way,' he said. 'I saw it just now. Some of you did too. It's not world-ending. Just, you know, another after-shock from the big one earlier tonight. But we've got a few minutes.'

The chant struck up again. 'QUAKE! QUAKE! QUAKE! QUAKE!'

Phaedra took this as her cue to move. Shikha couldn't see how she could prevail without a mic, but she opened her arms to the crowd below, glow globe in one hand, and sailed into a central spot, like a diva commanding the stage. She lifted the glow globe so that it shone down on her and seemed to shine through her. Again, the crowd stilled. Phaedra's voice rang clear across the plaza. 'This is our time! Don't believe the deceivers! No one owns us! No corporation has power over us. We govern ourselves! Just as you will govern yourselves. Transformation is coming! It's coming now!'

'Incredible,' said Morgan at Shikha's back. 'The woman believes her own bullshit.'

'QUAKE! QUAKE! QUAKE! QUAKE!'

Phaedra called out, 'HOLD!' and there was quiet again. She walked across to Jonah and began circling him. 'It's my own sweet glimpse boy,' she said, smiling, as though she had a plan and Jonah had walked right into it. She leaned close and gently pushed the mic he was holding away, then she spoke in a low murmur that Shikha strained to hear.

'You want this crowd? I can give them to you. They don't care what your GlimpseCorp man had to say. They're still mine. Whatever you want them to do, they'll do for me. Storm City Hall? They'll do that. Take on the BCB? They'll do that too. Hound the local gangsters out of town? Join us, and consider it done.' The crowd stirred, murmuring, waiting, uncertain about what was going on.

'They're not yours,' said Jonah. He turned to the crowd and spoke into the mic. 'They've promised you everything, haven't they. Even to bring back your dead. But you'll know by morning that it's all a lie.'

Phaedra walked back to Damon, took his hand and raised both their arms in a victory salute. The crowd cheered and Shikha could see Phaedra thinking, *Mine, all mine,* and feared this might be true.

But Jonah went on, 'I brought someone back from the dead tonight. He's right down there. And he's got a helluva story to tell about PANN and their promises.' He turned to Brett. 'Do you want to hear it?'

Phaedra's arms came down and her gaze found Bas and rested on him. He stared back at her, his face grazed and anguished. Phaedra's smile faded.

Brett started towards Jonah, shouting, 'All right, all right, that's enough. Give me back that mic.'

But suddenly Carlos was standing between Brett and Jonah. 'We are going to hear what the boy has to say.'

Brett blustered and Phaedra tossed her head and turned with Damon towards the church doors, but her attempts to retreat into the church were blocked by the gospel choir, lined up, unmoving, across the porch.

Bas had climbed the steps and taken the mic from Jonah. He turned to Phaedra and Damon. His voice was rasping and quiet but by now the crowd was quiet too, leaning in to hear.

'You promised me a new world,' said Bas. 'Didn't happen. You promised me my family back. That didn't happen either. You asked me about quake-prone build-ings, important buildings that might come down in a giant shake. And I didn't understand why you wanted to know, but I told you some, because I believed. I believed in you. I believed in your promise that we could be a new nation.

'Then I found out what you were really doing. You were going to bring those buildings down because you knew your giant quake prediction was a lie. You didn't care if there were people inside or nearby. You didn't care that those buildings might be important to us.

'And when I told someone what you were planning,' Bas went on, 'you decided to get rid of me. You thought you could make me vanish and no one would ever find me because I'd be buried under the train station that you destroyed.' He turned to the crowd. 'I can take you there, show you the hood they put over my head, and the ties they used to keep me there.' He bared his arm and held it up to show the welt the ties had made on his wrist. 'And Jonah has photos of the explosives in all those buildings that came down tonight.'

Bas turned back to the siblings. 'Do you hear my voice? It's rough because I screamed myself hoarse for someone to hear me. And someone did. You thought we didn't matter because we're just illegals. You thought no one had my back. You were wrong.'

Silence across the crowd and on the steps.

Then Bas turned away and handed the mic back to Jonah and went down to stand with Art.

Damon pointed towards him and shouted, 'Lies! All lies!' But the accusation sounded weak and empty now.

Shikha thought about how many people in the crowd had known Bas since he was a kid, and had known his mother and little sister. Doubt began to appear on the torchlit faces below.

Jonah turned to the crowd. 'You want transformation? Look around. There's no transformation here except the one we make ourselves. Their great transformation?' He pointed at Phaedra and Damon. 'It's never coming. You know that. They'll destroy the buildings we have left to make it look real, but it's fake all the way. You know and I know that PANN isn't here for us. It never was. PANN works for GlimpseCorp. And what does GlimpseCorp want? Not our recovery, that's for sure!'

The crowd murmured.

'But this is our place!' said Jonah. 'We're rebuilding it from rubble. And now GlimpseCorp wants to take the one thing that we have and they don't. Our glimpsing. Do we offer that up? To them? So that they can take it and cash in on it and walk away rich? Is that what you want?'

There was shouting now. 'NO! NO WAY!'

'Okay,' said Jonah. 'Let's do this instead.' He looked into Brett's camera. 'We're going to City Hall. We're not going to storm it. We're going to walk in there and we're going to say to them, and to all of you watching out there: "You want glimpsing? You want to be warned when a quake's on the way? Well, good, because we got that." There's plenty of people here who saw all the quakes tonight—you saw them coming, right?'

Loud cries of 'Yes!'

'Here's the deal,' said Jonah. He turned back to the camera. 'We'll warn you when there's a quake on the way but only if, first, the BCB stands down—that means no more raids, and it means bringing our people back from Flint Point. And second, City Hall helps us rebuild this place—that means rebuilding our houses and our shops and the mess that PANN made tonight. And if we get those things, if you help us be safe in our place, then we'll warn you so that you can be safe in yours.'

He looked around until he found Evie. She smiled and gave him two thumbs up.

Then the quake arrived, a rumbling, roaring, people-scattering shake. The plaza became a yelling mass of people cramming themselves into the holo field.

Shikha and Morgan both hit the ground, hands over heads.

When the earth stopped bucking and rolling, Shikha sat up and saw that Jonah and Evie hadn't moved. Nor had Phaedra and Damon but now they had Carlos at their back. Down in the plaza people began emerging from their huddles. Brett picked himself up, snatched the mic back from Jonah and turned to his camera. 'Well, folks, that's all from me. I hope you made it through tonight safe. We'll be back with another Glimpse Show next week. Take care and good night.' Brett tossed the mic to one of his technicians. 'Let's get out of here.'

Morgan said to him, 'We should look for Bev. She's down there somewhere.'

'Bev is great at looking after herself. As for you, I don't give a shit what you do now, you sure don't have a job anymore. And if, by some miracle, you do, I'm going to make it a waking nightmare.' He looked around at his crew. 'I'm off. If you want to come, then hurry it up.' He grabbed his bag and stormed away.

Morgan watched him go and began to say something to Shikha but she didn't hear it because right then three loud bangs came from inside the church, followed by a deafening explosion with a brilliant flash of light. Smoke came billowing out of the doorway and suddenly people were pointing and shouting and rushing towards the church and away from it, yelling 'FIRE! FIRE!'

Shikha found herself being rushed down the steps and then she got lost in the tumult of the crowd. She pushed and shoved her way through looking for Evie or Jonah or Morgan. Behind her, the church erupted into flames with a 'whump' that pushed waves of heat out into the plaza.

After a few moments of being jostled Shikha found a small space to stop under a linden tree and she stood there watching the flames. Then, with the crowd beginning to thin, she began to wander, still looking for Jonah or Evie or Bas. She almost fell over Morgan. He was kneeling on the ground staring at his hands, which had somehow turned black.

Shikha crouched beside him. 'What is it? What's the matter?'

'I…I …' He slumped to the ground.

'What's wrong?' she cried.

He was lying on his back, his face pale and frowning.

'Tell me!' She was angry now. 'Morgan? Come on! What's wrong?' Then she saw the dark shape spreading on his chest where his coat had fallen open.

He frowned up at her, gave a surprised little smile and murmured, 'She sent them for me after all.' His breathing bubbled on his lips, his head slumped to one side and his eyes grew still and blank.

Shikha knelt on the snowy ground, frozen with astonishment. She tugged at his coat, saying, 'No, no, no.' She looked frantically around for help but people were still racing around in a frenzy. Then Evie was there, and Jonah and Bas. Evie knelt down. 'Shikha? Mr Morgan?'

'He's…he's…' Shikha stammered and couldn't go on.

Evie lifted his coat, searching, touched blood-soaked cloth, stared at her fingers. The blood was seeping onto the snow now. 'I think he's been stabbed,' she said. She pressed her fingers on Morgan's neck, then she knelt back, staring at Shikha.

'Is he…' Shikha couldn't say the words. He couldn't be. He was just talking to her a few moments ago.

'He's dead,' said Evie. 'I'm so sorry.' They knelt in silent disbelief while the crowd charged around them. Then Evie reached over and closed Morgan's eyes.

Behind them the church was well ablaze, its rotten timbers burning hard. Flames leapt high into the sky until, at last, with a roar, the roof fell in and the building collapsed with a belch of hot, ashen air and a shudder like an earthquake.

The holos flickered and went out.

They ran from the howl of rage and despair that swept the plaza as the holos disappeared. The Ditz's lieutenant, Carlos, surprised Shikha by appearing from nowhere, and surprised her even more by picking Morgan up as easily as a man picks up a gun. He carried the dead man to the all-night clinic where a deeply weary medic sighed and said, 'Bring him in.' She looked at him then said, 'Evie honey, there's paperwork for this but we can't manage that right now—we've got a queue a mile long. We'll sort it in the morning. Come back then.'

'But what about the police?' said Shikha. 'I mean, he's been stabbed…'

'That's right.' The woman's tone was resigned. 'Stabbed in the middle of a riot in the middle of the D-Zone. What d'you think the police are gonna do?'

'He was a whistle-blower,' said Shikha. 'Someone should investigate.'

The receptionist shook her head. 'I'm sure someone should. But it won't be us, honey, and it won't be here.' She looked over Shikha's shoulder to the queue forming behind her then raised her eyebrows at Evie.

Evie led Shikha outside and sat her down on a bench alongside people with casts on their arms and legs, black eyes and bandaged heads. She took Shikha's hand in both of hers while Shikha blinked away tears. 'He was afraid,' said Shikha.

'Of exposing GlimpseCorp?'

'Of the quakes. He had a panic attack in the basement.' She smeared tears across her cheeks. 'He was a bastard, but…oh, I don't know. He didn't have to say anything. He didn't have to go public but I pestered him to.' She started to cry.

Evie put her arms around her as she sobbed. 'Less of a bastard than you might think, then.'

After a moment, Shikha sat up and tried to stifle her sobs. 'They killed him.'

'Yes,' said Evie. 'Let's find the others.'

The snow had turned thin and icy. Back towards the plaza the glow of the church on fire stained the clouds red but bands of would-be pilgrims still surged through the streets looking like they didn't want the party to end. Evie tucked her arm through Shikha's and hurried her along.

'Where are we going?' asked Shikha.

'Home.'

'Oh.'

A group of kids materialised out of the night, yelling and making faces at them, wild and random, then vanished again. Shikha flinched and stopped.

'Please,' said Evie. 'We should hurry.'

'What if they're after me too?'

'Shikha, please, let's keep moving.'

'But—'

'Later. We can talk about it later. Move, now. Move. That's it.'

But moving made Shikha feel far too visible; the world was swirling and dark and loud and the air smelled poisonously of smoke and ash. She stopped again as they were surrounded by another group and panic rose in her throat until she saw they were members of the choir. A thought arrived from what seemed like a vast distance to remind her that she hadn't slept in a long time and perhaps that was why the world was spinning and she was spinning with it, spinning and falling, spinning and falling, then she was looking up at Evie and the others, two of whom turned out to be Jonah and Bas, who were lifting her and helping her walk away from the noise and the crowds.

Shikha woke to find herself on a bed in a quiet room lit faintly by the glow of moonlight on snow. A small quake rolled through, jangling her nerves, and she waited to see if it was going to grow into something stronger, but it faded away.

'You okay?' said Evie's voice.

No, thought Shikha. A man died in front of me tonight. 'I can't make sense of it,' she whispered.

'Tomorrow,' said Evie. 'We'll make sense of it tomorrow.'

'Where are we?'

'We're home. We're safe. You can sleep, now.'

33

JONAH SAT IN the dark and listened to Evie breathe. The others had gone to bed, exhausted, but Jonah and Evie had sat on the couch in the common room reliving everything that had happened, moment by moment. Now Evie was sleeping, her head on Jonah's shoulder.

He was exhausted too, but his thoughts were hectic and overwhelming. He was glad of the darkness and he wanted to wrap himself in it and use it as a shield against people looking for him and at him, expecting him to do the next needful thing. It had been strange standing up in front of everyone like that, challenging Phaedra, urging the crowd to think again. It had been exhilarating. And terrifying. Now he was glad to hide away here in the Matterhorn while he tried to work out how to handle it all. He kissed Evie lightly on the top of her head. She stirred and smiled and slept again.

Bas was asleep in their old room, safe. There would be justice for what they had done to Bas; Jonah would make sure there was. Evie was here, under his arm, safe. Shikha was upstairs, safe. So were the rest of the Matterhorn family: Evie's mother, aunts and uncles who formed the choir, and Jonah's mum. He'd checked in on her when they got home. She had stirred in her bed when he kissed her and he'd whispered, 'It'll be all right,' like he always did.

Sitting downstairs now, listening to Evie's gentle breathing, he thought about that habit of consoling words, a habit of hope that things would soon be back to normal. For the longest time, talking to her like that had meant, you'll soon be back to your old self. But she wouldn't be, and he realised now that he'd known that for years.

He sat and thought about her, living in her own quiet world, and about his dad who seemed just as distant, and he ached for them. The ache could not be reassured away, it could not be reasoned into nothing. Bas had taught him that. The ache was an ache and it was his. It was as simple as that, and as difficult. He knew that he'd been slow getting here, but here he was at last. He could not change what had happened; not his mother's injury, not his own stupid act of losing all that money. It was time, he knew, to stop pretending. Things would never go back to how they were before the quakes. He made himself sit in the dark and let that knowledge lie heavy on him.

Sometime in the night, Evie woke and sat up, then groaned and stood up. 'That is one ancient couch. My back's killing me.' She stretched and walked around the room, stopping to look out the window at the falling snow. When she came back to him she curled up beside him, looked at him closely and touched his cheek. 'Why are you sad?' She kissed him lightly. 'You found Bas. And you defeated PANN.'

'We,' he amended, 'maybe, partially, for a moment, derailed PANN slightly.'

'Pessimist,' she murmured with a smile.

'But yes,' he said, 'finding Bas was the best thing.'

Evie snuggled back beside him, put her arms around him and held him close. She hummed softly, stopping when a small quake rumbled through, then starting up again once it had gone. Eventually, her breathing slowed and deepened and she drifted back to sleep. Jonah watched her, mesmerised by how beautiful she was.

In the morning, Shikha wanted to go back to the clinic where they'd left Morgan's body hours earlier. 'I still can't believe it,' she said. 'Maybe he isn't really dead?'

But when they got there, the receptionist shook her head. 'Gone,' she said. 'People came from town. Authorised by the family. They had the documentation and they took him away.'

'But…but…' spluttered Shikha. 'You believed them?'

The woman on reception had the frazzled air of someone patching a puncture and finding new leaks with every patch. 'What am I gonna do, honey? They got the papers, they legit get the body.'

Shikha turned, open-mouthed, to Evie. 'But—'

Evie led her away. 'Nothing we can do about that now.'

The streets felt hungover. There were people about, but they seemed listless and pained, as though the day was too bright and the possibility of talking to anyone too awkward. The companionship of the night before was gone. Shikha and the others fell in with a straggle of people moving towards the plaza.

The church—what was left of it—was still smoking, a charred sore on the new-fallen snow. People were picking their way through the space where the holo shrine used to be, gathering up the toys and other small gifts that they had brought to their lost ones. The faint ghostly radiance the holos used to give off in the daylight was gone; the light in that space was flat and empty now. Some of the tech that generated each holo was still there, a lot of it scuffed up by the stampeding crowd of the night before, and some of it dug out and carried off.

Of Phaedra and Damon, there was no sign.

'Made a mess and ran away,' said Evie.

'Maybe,' said Jonah. 'Didn't Carlos have an eye on them?'

'He helped us with Morgan,' said Shikha. 'So I guess he took his eye off them.'

'Let's go and ask,' said Evie, with a smile.

The Ditz's place was decorated with a clean blanket of snow and icicles hanging from its eaves, but it looked just as menacing as usual. Carlos answered the door.

'Can we talk to—' began Jonah.

'She's not here,' said Carlos. 'Gone into town on business.'

'What business?' asked Evie. 'PANN? GlimpseCorp?'

Carlos raised an eyebrow.

'We were wondering,' said Jonah. 'About Phaedra and Damon and what happened to them last night?'

'Not my place to say,' said Carlos.

'Are they here?'

'No.'

'Are they still in the zone?'

'What is this? Twenty questions? Not as far as I know.' He started to close the door, then stopped and said, 'Their sort always survive. You know that, right? They crawl away and hide for a while, lick their wounds. Then out they come with a new identity and new ways of grift. Don't waste your time on them. They're not worth it.'

He moved to close the door. Jonah called out, 'Wait!

We wanted to say thanks. To you. And her. For believing us. And for stepping in. So…thanks.'

Carlos's face betrayed the hint of a smile. He gave a short nod. 'I'll tell her.' And he closed the door.

They stared at it for a while.

'This is not the end,' said Shikha. 'There's going to be a Glimpse Show that tells the story of what happened here. Bev might do it, but if she won't I'll go to Jericho— they're the competition. They'll be interested. Someone will want to tell this story. And if they won't, I will. I'm gonna be a director. Sooner than you think.'

Evie laughed. 'All power to you,' she said as they turned away and walked back towards the Matterhorn.

NEWS @ EIGHT
GLIMPSE GAMBLE FALLS FLAT

Say what you like about GlimpseCorp—they think BIG. But that all came to grief last night when their much heralded anniversary show turned upside-down in spectacular fashion. The anniversary special was expected to rescue GlimpseCorp from the death spiral of its ratings dive. It had everything: the dreaded D-Zone, a cult promising an anniversary miracle, a fugitive young glimpser who may or may not have been planting explosives in quake-prone buildings. With material like that you'd expect a smash hit! And it was! Ratings were through the roof.

But then it fell apart.

How did a fun anniversary celebration turn into a series of demands from D-Zone residents for rebuilding their disaster-prone area? An unexpected and unwelcome ending by all accounts.

And it has come to light that the group, People for a New Nation, is in the pay of GlimpseCorp, so it seems the whole show was rigged from the start.

Facing a barrage of legal challenges from people who lost out betting big on whether something major was going to occur last night, as promised by New Nation leaders, GlimpseCorp CEO Kerryn Duval had this to say: 'I'm aware that some people are unhappy, but I urge them to realise that we are in the entertainment business. What did you expect?'

Asked about the midnight riot and the destruction of a number of buildings in the area, including a church, Ms Duval agreed that this was unfortunate. The riot claimed at least one life, according to health workers in the Zone. Ms Duval denied all knowledge. 'No, I'm not aware of this. Obviously, it's a tragic outcome which the GlimpseCorp team would have tried to prevent had it been possible.'

Asked about future plans, Ms Duval said, 'The Glimpse Show will return, bigger and better than ever. Yes, I do know that GlimpseCorp shares are sliding on the back of the rumour that the glimpses are fading. What nonsense! Didn't you see that boy last night? GlimpseCorp has ample reserves of glimpsers. I guarantee it. Watch this space!'

Meanwhile, complaints are growing daily that with its mostly illegal population, the D-Zone has a better quake-warning system in place than City Hall is providing for legitimate city dwellers. Another quake struck this afternoon. Here in the city we were taken unawares, but people in the D-Zone had enough warning to safeguard themselves and their loved ones from danger. Their representatives told News@Eight that their offer still stands: release those detained by the Border Control Bureau at Flint Point and begin the long-delayed rebuild of Downtown East, then they'll share their glimpsing with the city.

What's the status of these negotiations? Is the city any closer to the restoration of a quake-warning system? We contacted City Hall for comment. Mayor Norton Stavers is adamant that the city will not negotiate with illegals. But he will have to. And he'd better move fast. City residents have immediate and urgent concerns about their lives and liveli-hoods. Now is not the time to play politics.

34

'NICE VIEW,' SAID the Detective Inspector. 'Thirty-nine floors, is it? Impressive. On base isolators, I believe? A safe place to be in a quake, then. Now, we have a few questions for you, Ms Duval. We're investigating the disappearance of one Phillip Morgan. Known to you, I believe?'

'No, not really.'

She hadn't stood up to greet them. She wondered if she should have. Did one normally stand to greet the police? Perhaps. She hadn't any experience in such matters. They were talking again.

'We have a witness statement that Phillip Morgan was stabbed in the plaza of Downtown East on the night of—'

'Yes, yes, the night of the anniversary.' She realised too late that she shouldn't have jumped to that night so quickly. And interrupted him! She shouldn't have interrupted him. She wanted them gone.

'That's correct, Ms Duval, the night of the anniversary.'

She stood up and walked to the window—this is what she did when members of the board came to see her. She liked that they had to look at her framed by the great sweep of the city. Today, though, it made her feel small. Thirty-nine floors below her, the camp of news media on the steps of the building hadn't got any smaller. They'd been there since it all began to turn south—since Morgan spewed it all out in a tirade that had turned her skin clammy and her stomach sick. She couldn't see why people were making such a fuss. So what, if they'd had a few conversations with PANN and with City Hall? So what, if some money had changed hands to make things run a little more smoothly? She was doing everyone a service by seeking out genuine glimpsers. But people had turned on her. The share price was in freefall.

'Look, officer—'

'Detective Inspector.'

'My apologies, Detective Inspector.' She'd got that wrong. Had he introduced himself? Yes, of course he had. And she'd been too rattled to take it in. 'Detective Inspector, I understand that there was a riot that night. Of course, people were injured. I can hardly be held responsible for the risks that a former employee chose to expose himself to. Now, if you will just—'

'Ms Duval, we have documentation indicating that

Phillip Morgan was, until the night in question, an employee of Glimpse Corporation, and we have four further witness statements that explicate a longstanding and close working relationship between you and Mr Morgan.'

Four! How dare they? No one was loyal anymore. 'I really don't think—'

'Ms Duval, you'll have to accompany us to the station for a full statement. Now. Thank you.'

35

HOTEL DIRAC WAS still standing. Last Chance Jackson was still sitting in an old armchair in a corner of the atrium, still petting the cat, still smoking something foul. He smiled at Jonah and Bas.

'Lift's out. I think you knew that.'

'I figured,' said Jonah.

'But as you see'——Chance tipped an imaginary cap towards them both——'we're still here. I tell you…when that lass…'

'Evie.'

'When Evie came charging in here the day before the anniversary yelling that we were all gonna be blown to kingdom come on account of explosives hidden somewhere here by the PANN crazies, well, to be honest with you, I thought she was high.' He shook his head. 'Turns out, not.'

'No,' said Jonah. 'It was all real. You found some-thing then.'

'Oh, yes. Yes, indeed, we did. A big package of bad stuff in the basement, all wired and ready to blow us all sky-high. Would've been the end of this old place once and for all. We even, courtesy of the Lady Alphonsine, got the cops in to take a look, dust for fingerprints, that kind of thing.' He shook his head again. 'I tell you, I'm still struggling to believe it.'

'Cops took you seriously?' asked Jonah.

'They took the Lady Al very seriously. So seriously, in fact, that I do wonder about her. What's she got on them? What does she know? *Who* does she know? But then, I think to myself, Chance, that's above your pay grade. Just enjoy being in the orbit of that woman's mysterious power.'

Jonah laughed. 'Is she in?'

'I believe she is. Go on up.'

As they climbed the stairs, Jonah said to Bas, 'You okay?'

'Sure.'

Bas had been quiet in the few days since the anni-versary pandemonium, as Jonah had taken to calling it. And Jonah and Evie hadn't pressed him to talk. They'd left him to sleep and eat and when he wasn't sleeping they were relieved that he would sit at the kitchen table and listen to them make plans about what to do next, how to talk to City Hall.

That Bas had wanted to come to Dirac, Jonah took to be a good sign.

They reached the fifth level and Jonah knocked on the door of Alphonsine's apartment. She opened it, smiling.

'Jonah. Sebastian. Come in.'

When they were sitting at her table she produced chocolates on a silver tray and coffee in a silver pot. 'I want to thank you both most profoundly on behalf of everyone living here,' she said. 'Our beloved Dirac is still standing, and this is down to the warning we received from Evie.'

'And Bas,' said Jonah. 'He nearly died for letting us know.'

Bas cleared his throat. 'I'm here to say sorry. You were only in danger because of me. Because I picked the buildings for them to target. I didn't know what they were going to do, but still, you could all have died! And I'm sorry. I'm so sorry.'

It was the most Bas had said in days. Jonah watched him and knew that there was a long way to go. But he also knew that Bas would make it okay. He was a fighter. And here was a different kind of fight than he was used to: to move on from the madness of being swallowed up by PANN and come back to being himself again.

Alphonsine was shaking her head. 'As you say, you

didn't know what they were planning. And as soon as you found out, you tried to stop it.'

'But you could have all died!' said Bas again.

'And yet, here we are. You have exposed PANN for what they are, at great risk to yourself.'

'And we have to make that count,' said Jonah. 'Something has to happen out of all this to make a difference.'

'Oh, I think something will certainly happen,' said Alphonsine.

'Only if we can negotiate with City Hall to rebuild here in return for offering them our glimpsing. But we don't know how to do that. We don't know anything about politics or making deals with the city. We've got people who glimpse and that's it. What do we do now?' He tried the coffee. It was black and hot and very strong. 'We need people who know City Hall and how to talk to them. Will you help us?'

Alphonsine smiled. 'Help you strike a deal with City Hall? Of course. I would be pleased to do that.'

They had talked about this, Jonah and Evie, with Bas listening in, and they had decided to ask some people for help. Evie's mother, for a start, who knew her way around campaigns. And Alphonsine. And maybe even Ditz Carmichael. Now, with Alphonsine answering him so positively, Jonah felt a surge of confidence that they might at least make a dent in City Hall's long-held resolve to ignore the D-Zone.

Jonah nodded. 'Thank you. There's one other thing. Last time I was here—' he half smiled, '—you said that if I made it through the anniversary, you'd arrange a loan so I can pay Shikha back for those ID papers.'

Alphonsine laughed, a long peal of delight. 'Jonah. Have you always asked so little of the world? We owe everything to the two of you and Evie. Our home here, our lives. Is this all you are asking for? Some help with City Hall and a small loan?' She shook her head. 'You can ask for more than that.'

He was uncertain how to answer her. He said, 'You might have found out about the explosives before it all went up. Didn't Chance see anything?'

'Chance.' She puffed on an imaginary cigarette. 'Chance is not always with us, if you know what I mean. No. We would not have known until it was too late. And that being so, I will not give you that loan. Let me tell you this instead. These People for a New Nation, Phaedra and Damon and their little band of helpers, who ran away last night—they took a small fortune from loyal followers. They've been doing that for years. I think you know this. Now they will find, when they go looking, that their bank accounts are closed to them. And when they pursue the matter to prise them open, they will find that they are all empty.

'Now, I believe they owe your family at least fifteen thousand dollars?' She smiled at the expression on Jonah's face. 'I'm sure you would like that back. I will arrange it.'

Jonah and Bas came out of Dirac into sunshine. 'What do you want to do?' asked Jonah.

Bas stood still and raised his face, eyes closed, to the sun. The scar on his cheek was healing. His hair was growing out of the pilgrim cut. 'First, find some food,' he said. 'I'm starving. And then, get to work.'

They walked back into the D-Zone. 'I'm with you on the food,' said Jonah. 'But what work do you mean?'

'Work in the real world,' said Bas. 'There's a few battles ahead, right? I want to start rebuilding this place with the people who live here. I want to make it safe for everyone.'

ACKNOWLEDGMENTS

I wrote and rewrote this book more times than I want to count in the years following the quakes that roared through my city of Ōtautahi Christchurch in 2010–2012. For their friendship, counsel and generosity during this strange time, enduring thanks to Hugh Campbell, Marion Familton, Jill Hawkey, Lucy D'Aeth, Barbara and Graeme Nicholas, Kathleen Rushton, Joanna Orwin and, always, to Paul Dalziel. Thanks to Jane Pearson for her editorial wisdom and to the team at Text who welcomed me back after years away. Lastly, I, and many others, owe a debt of gratitude to the people of our city who, through their kindness, creativity and perseverance, have worked staunchly towards a just rebuild. Kia kaha e hoa mā!